"I'm
Tess Montg...
"Is S... ...ome?"

The girl shook her dark head. "Not yet," she said.

"Do you mind if I wait?"

She ran her tongue across her lips. "You can wait," she said.

Noah crutched his way through the snow and opened the gate. He smiled at the girl. An ally.

She turned back to look at him again as he shut the gate, her scrutiny so intense it was a little unnerving.

"Nice snowman," he said.

"Thanks."

"I'm Noah Tanner," he said, realizing she had no idea who he was.

"I know."

"You do?" Amazing. How many girls her age knew a world champion bronc rider when they saw one? "Did Tess tell you about me?"

She nodded solemnly.

He grinned, pleased as punch. "You really know who I am?"

"You're my father," she said.

Dear Reader,

As a very special treat this season, Silhouette Desire is bringing you the best in holiday stories. It's our gift from us—the editorial staff at Silhouette—to you, the readers. The month begins with a very special MAN OF THE MONTH from Ann Major, *A Cowboy Christmas*. Years ago, a boy and girl were both born under the same Christmas star. She grew up rich; he grew up poor...and when they met, they fell into a love that would last a lifetime....

Next, Anne McAllister's CODE OF THE WEST series continues with *Cowboys Don't Stay,* the third book in her series about the Tanner brothers.

Christmas weddings are always a lot of fun, and that's why we're bringing you *Christmas Wedding* by Pamela Macaluso. And if Texas is a place you'd like to spend the holidays—along with a sexy Texas man—don't miss *Texas Pride* by Barbara McCauley. Next, popular Silhouette Romance writer Sandra Steffen makes her Desire debut with *Gift Wrapped Dad*.

Finally, do not miss *Miracles and Mistletoe,* another compelling love story from the talented pen of Cait London.

So, from our "house" to yours...Happy Holidays.

Lucia Macro

Please address questions and book requests to:
Silhouette Reader Service
U.S.: 3010 Walden Ave., P.O. Box 1325, Buffalo, NY 14269
Canadian: P.O. Box 609, Fort Erie, Ont. L2A 5X3

ANNE McALLISTER
COWBOYS DON'T STAY

SILHOUETTE *Desire*®

Published by Silhouette Books

America's Publisher of Contemporary Romance

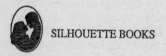

SILHOUETTE BOOKS

ISBN 0-373-05969-8

COWBOYS DON'T STAY

Printed in U.S.A.

Books by Anne McAllister

Silhouette Desire

*Cowboys Don't Cry #907
*Cowboys Don't Quit #944
*Cowboys Don't Stay #969

*Code of the West

ANNE McALLISTER

was born and raised in California, land of surfers, swimmers and beach-volleyball players. She spent her teenage years researching them in hopes of finding the perfect hero. It turned out, however, that a few summer weeks spent at her grandparents' in Colorado and all those hours in junior high spent watching Robert Fuller playing Jess Harper on "Laramie" were formative. She was fixated on dark, handsome, intense, lone-wolf types. Twenty-six years ago she found the perfect one prowling the stacks of the university library and married him. They now have four children, three dogs, a fat cat and live in the Midwest (as in "Is this heaven?" "No, it's Iowa.") in a reasonable facsimile of semiperfect wedded bliss to which she always returns—even though the last time she was in California she had lunch with Robert Fuller.

The fourth installment of CODE OF THE WEST— Taggart Jones's story—will be coming to you in the summer of 1996. Watch for THE COWBOY AND THE KID—only from Silhouette Desire!

For Robert Fuller,
my second cowboy hero.

For Ronnie Rondell and Buddy Phelps.
Imagine meeting you here,
or, if you don't find the dedication in one book,
look in the next one.
Better late than never, right, guys?

And for Linda Hender Wallerich,
aka Jessica Douglass,
who knows a hero when she sees one.

Prologue

"It's whiter'n a polar bear's insides out there," Noah Tanner said, squinting through the windshield. "Snow's so thick I can't see the damn road."

His callused fingers flexed on the steering wheel of the van he was driving, and not for the first time, he wished they were closer to home. Or to his brother's Wyoming ranch, which was where he was headed and which was a damn sight more cozy than the Colorado post-office box he was calling home these days. He put his foot down a little harder on the accelerator, hoping to get in a few more miles before the full brunt of the storm hit.

They'd been doing their best to outrun the storm since leaving Vegas yesterday evening. Taggart had bet him then that they'd beat it to Tanner's ranch near the Big Horns in Wyoming. Now Noah hoped to God he was right.

"I don't mind a white Christmas," Noah continued, "long as it waits awhile."

His traveling partner, Taggart Jones, grinned confidently. "It will. What snowstorm would dare fly in the face of two world champions?"

At that Noah grinned, too—a grin still three parts amazement to one part satisfaction that, when the NFR finals had ended the day before, they'd both come out on top. Taggart Jones had become the Professional Rodeo Cowboy Association's bull-riding champion of the year. And two time second-place finisher, Noah Tanner, was this time—finally, at last—the PRCA champion bronc rider.

"Reckon you're right," he said, flicking a glance down at the shiny new gold buckle holding up his Wranglers.

But as the snow continued to swirl thickly around the van and the lanes of the interstate disappeared beneath the accumulation, Noah turned his attention back to the road and didn't feel quite so sure.

"We'll be fine," Taggart said. "Gotta be. Becky's Christmas program is tomorrow morning and I told her I'd be there. So come hell or high water—or snowstorms—I'm gonna be."

"Course you are," Noah agreed. If anybody could get through, they could. In the years he'd been going down the road from one rodeo to the next, the cumulative hours he'd spent on Interstate 80 figured in the weeks, if not the months by now. He reckoned he ought to know it by heart.

"It's the first year she hasn't been with me in Vegas since she was born," Taggart went on glumly.

Noah knew that the one blight on Taggart's otherwise fantastic finals was the fact that his six-year-old daughter had missed it because she was in school full-time now.

"She's gonna be madder'n a bee-stung pony if she missed it and then I miss her Christmas program, too," Taggart said as he rubbed the back of his neck, then grinned wryly. "Promising in blood to be back in time for her program was the only way I could stop her sneaking off and hitching a ride down.''

Noah grinned, too, at the notion of a six-year-old enterprising enough to find her way from Montana to Las Vegas. Still, he'd known Becky Jones since she was hatched, and if anyone could do it, headstrong, tomboy Becky was the one.

"If we make Tan—um, Robert and Maggie's before dawn, you'll be there in time."

Taggart's mouth quirked into a grin. "Still can't get used to him bein' Robert. Hell, he was Tanner for years."

He still was, in Noah's mind, though Noah was doing his best to remember his brother had another name. "Since he met Maggie, he's Robert. Well broke and lovin' every minute of it. Shoulda heard him when I called to tell him I won. He was excited enough, but I think tellin' me about Jared sittin' his new pony excited him a damn sight more." Jared was Robert and Maggie's two-and-a-half-year-old son, and even though he had to share the limelight with twin brothers now, Jared was still quite definitely the apple of his father's eye.

"I can understand that," Taggart said. "Seein' Becky be a snowman in the play tomorrow's gonna thrill the heck outa me." He stared out the windshield at the swirling snow and added reflectively, "More'n winning did."

And the damnedest thing was, Noah knew he was telling the truth.

"Reckon I must be missin' something," he said, then slanted Taggart a grin. "I'm sure as hell gonna be out of place at Christmas this year—the lone bachelor. Good grief, Tan—I mean Robert and Maggie, have three little curtain climbers now, and Luke and Jill have one. Reckon I oughta find myself a woman and have one of my own?"

"Don't rush things," Taggart counseled. "It ain't healthy." His own grin was weary and more than a little sad. "I oughta know."

That was true enough. Seven years ago, Taggart had rushed things. He'd met a bright-eyed, big-city girl in a funky New York restaurant after the rodeo in Madison Square Garden and had swept her off her feet. Julie Westmore had never known a "real live cowboy before."

They'd had less than forty-eight hours together before Taggart had had to board a plane west. But in the time they did have, he'd fallen head over heels with an equally love-struck Julie. In the next three weeks he'd spent a fortune on long-distance phone calls—as many as it took to convince Julie to marry him.

In December she had. Ten months later she'd had Becky—and by Christmas she'd left them.

She hadn't had a clue about what marrying a rodeo cowboy entailed. She couldn't stand following her husband down the road, and she'd had no desire to wait at home with a baby while he made a living the only way he knew how.

"We have nothing in common!" she'd screamed at Taggart the night after he got back from the National Finals six years before. Noah, who'd retreated to the other bedroom, had heard her loud and clear—the same way he'd heard the door slam, the footsteps running down the stairs and the wail of two-month-old Becky, left in her father's arms.

"She'll be back," Taggart had said hollowly the next morning.

But she hadn't been. Julie had got a divorce without ever seeing either her husband or her daughter again.

"It's just as well," Taggart had said on one of the rare occasions when he even talked about Julie. He and Noah had been spending a few days at Taggart's parents' house north of Bozeman last winter. It had been a snowy afternoon, with not much to do but loaf around the house and drink beer and get under Mrs. Jones's feet. "Julie was right, you know. We didn't belong together. Still—" and here he'd paused and glanced back at his five-year-old daughter, who was playing with her toy horses in the middle of the living room floor "—I reckon it was worth it. She gave me Becky."

"Becky's a goer," Noah said now, and he smiled at the way Taggart's pained smile turned into a real one.

"She's some kid, all right. Chip off the old block." The smile became a grin and he laughed as he looked over at Noah. "Did I tell you she wants to ride bulls?"

Wind buffeted the van. In the rearview mirror, Noah could see a semi looming through the worsening snow. "You gonna let her?"

"Hell, no," Taggart said promptly. "I'm not having any daughter of mine doin' anything that dangerous. She'd break her fool neck."

Noah laughed. "What's sauce for the gander..."

Taggart shook his head. "Don't you believe it. She can be a barrel racer if she wants to," he added magnanimously.

"Generous of you. Hell—" Noah glanced in the mirror again and sucked in his breath "—he'd better slow down."

"Who?"

Noah jerked his head. "That truck. He isn't gonna try to pass, is he?"

But clearly he was. And then he wasn't.

Trying to brake on the snow-covered road only made things worse. The semi didn't slow down; it began to slide sideways.

Noah saw it coming in the mirror. The side of the trailer, as red and cheerful as Christmas, swung around and in slow motion slid straight at them.

One

He wasn't dead.

At least that's what they told him.

They were probably right. Being dead, Noah figured, wouldn't hurt quite so much. Every bone, every muscle—hell, every hair on his head—hurt like sin.

He mustered all his strength and shifted his position in the bed about an inch. At least there was nothing wrong with his memory. He knew exactly what had happened. He could still see it in his mind's eye—the truck trailer slapping into the van like Ken Griffey, Jr., ripping into a fast ball. Noah felt like the cover, torn right off the ball.

He couldn't believe he'd really ridden nine out of ten NFR broncs just last week. It didn't seem possible. At the moment lifting his head didn't seem possible.

At least he could breathe. He could remember a time—just *when* was a little hazy, though—when even getting air seemed an iffy proposition.

It was because of his collapsed lung, he remembered them telling him. And that was because of his four broken ribs. And they were the result of that trailer playing baseball with the van, whacking him and Taggart clear out of the park.

Where the hell was Taggart? Noah couldn't remember having seen him since the accident, not since the paramedics had arrived and removed his friend's unconscious body from the van.

And that had been . . . when? He didn't know. He didn't know where he was—some hospital in Laramie? Cheyenne?—or how long he'd been here. Hell, and he'd thought his memory was all right?

He didn't know anything!

"*Taggart!*" Noah struggled to sit up. All his muscles screamed.

"Here now. It's all right." The voice came from the left. It was soft, soothing. Gentle. Female. "It's okay, Noah. It's okay."

At the sound of his name, Noah tried to turn his head. Other muscles protested. He groaned and his head fell back against the pillow.

"Your friend's all right. Take it easy," the voice said again, and a nurse came into his range of vision. A slender nurse in a starchy white uniform. A nurse with oddly familiar, wide green eyes and dark brown hair that was pulled back into a long braid. An even-longer braid than he remembered.

Noah stared, disbelieving.

"*T-Tess?*" It took him a minute to find enough air to form her name.

"Hello, Noah."

He smiled weakly and a little wryly. "What is this—déjà vu?"

A faint smile crossed her face. "Not quite." Her voice was soft, but her tone was neutral, professional. That wasn't the way it had been . . . how long ago? Seven years? Eight?

Even though, of course, it was how they had met. She'd been studying to become a nurse and was doing a practicum in the hospital where he ended up after getting hung up and kicked and concussed at the Laramie rodeo. He'd barely regained consciousness when his buddies had left him and headed down the road again. The next day, he'd been well enough to leave, but had had nowhere to go.

After a moment's indecision that was reflected clearly on her face, the dark-haired, starry-eyed nursing student he'd flirted with since they'd carried him into the hospital had agreed to take him home.

She wasn't the sort of girl he normally hung around with. The brash, eager "buckle bunnies" who generally followed him around were a far cry from the serious girl who had told him her name was Tess Montgomery.

Tess Montgomery had been thin and coltish, shy, yet surprisingly eager to please. She had also been the most beautiful girl he'd ever seen.

She still was. But there was no eagerness about her now, nor shyness, either—only a pleasant smile and cool, professional competence.

She was Tess Montgomery, R.N.—the first and last woman with whom he'd had what could even remotely be called "an affair." Tess Montgomery—one of the many women he'd loved and left. Tess Montgomery—the only woman who'd ever cried when he'd walked out the door.

God had one heck of a sense of humor, was all Noah could think.

What Tess thought, he didn't know. She was all business as she checked the tube in his chest that they'd put in when they'd reinflated his lung. When she was done, she listened with a stethoscope. He opened his mouth to say something.

She popped a thermometer in.

"Tess—"

"Shh." She moved to the foot of the bed and jotted something on his chart. He watched her. She used to smile at him, then, if he winked, look quickly away. Today there were no smiles—not after that first meant-to-be-reassuring one. He was just another patient now. In fact, it was probably worse. Maybe she hated him.

Naw, she couldn't. Could she? He wondered if he ought to ask. It didn't seem like the best place to start a conversation.

He shifted the thermometer. "Is Taggart...?"

"He's fine and he's right down the hall. Now hush." She went back to writing, ignoring him once more.

Noah scowled. "What's the matter with him?"

She glared. "He's doing fine," she repeated.

"He was unconscious!"

"Noah—"

"Tell me, damn it."

"I'll tell you," Tess said with exaggerated patience, "*if* you keep your mouth shut." And she closed her own mouth in a firm line, waiting until he slumped back against his pillows in acquiescence. Then she nodded, satisfied. "Your friend has a broken femur, two cracked ribs and a concussion. And yes, he stayed unconscious for most of yesterday, but he's awake now and quite coherent. More than you've been."

Noah frowned. How long had he been out of it, then? "When was it—th'accident, I mean?"

"Noah!"

"S'rry," he muttered around the thermometer, looking as abashed as he could.

At last she took pity on him. "The accident was yesterday afternoon. It's now almost 3:00 p.m. Tuesday."

He opened his mouth.

"And if you say another word, Noah, I will walk out of here and send Nurse Long Needle back in my place. And don't think I won't."

He hadn't known Tess long, but he'd known her well. She would do it. He fumed in silence while she took his blood pressure, shined a penlight into his eyes and shut it off again, then wrote some more. After about four hundred years, she took the thermometer out of his mouth.

"Nurse Long Needle?" He arched a sceptical brow.

"She's Cheyenne."

He didn't believe a word of it. "Behave, you mean?"

"Behave," Tess agreed.

Noah looked down at his aching body. His right shoulder and elbow were strapped against his torso. His ribs weren't taped, but they weren't exactly eager to go anywhere. He had a tube in his chest. His knee was immobilized in ice. There was an IV running from his left hand to a bag hanging by the bed. "I can't do anything else," he grumbled. "I want to see Taggart."

"By all means. Just hop right up and go down the hall. Room 218."

"Sarcasm, Tess?"

"Common sense, Noah."

He considered that, considered how far away the door was, considered how far away the floor was, for that matter. "You're probably right," he muttered after a moment. "So, when can I see him?"

"A day or so. Ask your doctor."

"Who *is* my doctor?" Hell, there was a whole world of stuff he didn't know.

"Dr. Alvarez for your lung. Dr. MacGuinness for your ribs and your knee and your elbow and shoulder."

"Do I have anything that isn't under a doctor's care?" he asked wryly.

Tess smiled. "Not much. You can have a pain pill if you want one. It's that time."

"Don't need one," he lied.

"Suit yourself." Tess started toward the door.

"Tess!" He levered himself up as far as he could.

She turned, one hand on the doorjamb. Her braid, he could see now, reached past the middle of her back. He remembered how her hair had looked fanned out against the white sheet. He remembered how soft it had felt to his touch. He swallowed.

"Are you . . . mad at me?"

She stared at him. "Mad?" Tess said. "No." She shook her head slowly. Her eyes met his for one long moment before her gaze flickered down briefly, then came up to meet his again. A faint smile touched the corners of her mouth. "Actually, Noah, I owe you a debt of gratitude."

There. She'd seen him—conscious and coherent this time—and she'd escaped unscathed. She'd even managed to be professional and polite.

It didn't matter that her hands were shaking as she walked down the hall to the nurse's station. It didn't matter that her breakfast was doing somersaults in her stomach and that there was a lump the size of a Rocky Mountain in her throat.

He didn't know that. And that was what mattered. That, and that she manage to keep her indifference firmly in place until Noah Tanner was once more out of her life.

"What's the matter?" Nita LongReach asked her. "You look like you've gone ten rounds with a ghost."

Tess shook her head and managed a wan smile. "Just hungry," she lied, knowing full well she'd upchuck if she even caught a whiff of a lunch tray right now. "I didn't eat lunch."

Nita grunted. "You work too hard."

"We all work too hard."

"But you more than most. You need a break. A vacation. A little joy in your life."

"I have a little joy in my life," Tess said. Her hands trembled less now. She wiped her palms surreptitiously on the sides of her white slacks.

"Besides Susannah," Nita said patiently. "You need more than a daughter and a job that takes all your time."

"Get a life, you mean?"

Nita grinned. "Get a man."

"No, thanks." Tess would have been far more emphatic if she thought Nita wouldn't accuse her of overreacting. She picked up a set of charts and riffled through them.

"Derek's interested." It hadn't gone unnoticed that earnest Derek Mallon, the new ob-gyn resident, seemed to be popping up everywhere Tess Montgomery went. "Either that or he's lost an awful lot of the time." Nita giggled. "Why else would he end up in orthopedics so often?"

"Maybe he's interested in you."

"I'm twenty years older than he is and fifty pounds heavier."

"Love is blind," Tess said blithely. It was also stupid, and dangerous to the heart, but she wasn't saying that.

"Well, if you don't want Derek, there're other fish in the sea. Want a cowboy?"

"*What?*" Tess almost dropped the charts in her hand.

Nita, noticing, looked speculative. "I'm not selling them, if that's what you're worried about. I just thought . . . what about either of those two rodeo cowboys? Handsome devils, both of 'em. They're a bit battered at the moment, but when the bruising fades..."

"No," Tess said flatly. "I don't want a cowboy." Never again.

A debt of gratitude?

The words tumbled around in Noah's head, mocking him. What the hell did that mean?

Because he'd destroyed her childish fantasies? Because he'd loved her and left her? Because he'd squashed her young girl's dreams and taught her what men were really like?

Or was she just being sarcastic?

Probably. Without a doubt he deserved it.

He took the pain pill after all. And four hours later another. And then another.

They muddled his mind as much as they dulled his pain. He dozed and dreamed, and in his mind he saw a million horses, a million rides, a million miles of road...and a million memories of Tess.

"Do you take in strays?" he'd asked her, only half-joking, the day he was to be discharged.

Her green eyes had widened perceptibly. She'd swallowed, then blinked. Then a shy smile had lit her face. "I believe I could."

So she had. He was broke and hungry, and his head still ached. She'd been kind, gentle, caring. She'd fussed over him with a tenderness he hadn't experienced since his mother had died, when he was four.

Maybe it was the care, maybe it was the concussion. Whatever the cause, she tapped a part of Noah that had lain dormant for so many years he'd totally forgotten it was there. He'd grown gentle, too, teasing her tenderly, smiling at her, laughing with her. Basking in the comfort of her concern.

He'd been on the road, without a family, for so long that all the TLC she was lavishing on him turned his head. It was wonderful. The picnics she took him on were fun. The hikes in the mountains and swims at the lake were fantastic.

But he wanted more. He was plagued with a young man's needs, a young man's lusts. And not too many days passed before Tess, overcoming her initial shyness, had satisfied them—had satisfied him.

For two weeks she welcomed him into her life, into her arms, into her bed. She gave him days of joy and nights of love.

Sometimes, lying next to her at night, he dreamed that he could have this paradise forever.

But in the clear light of day, he knew it couldn't last.

He was a rodeo bronc rider. A close-to-broke rodeo bronc rider. And the only way he could change that last fact was to get on down the road to more rodeos and leave Tess Montgomery behind.

Still, when his buddies came to pick him up on their way back to Cheyenne later that month, he'd felt a momentary pang. From the look on her face when he came out of the bedroom carrying his duffel bag and saddle, Tess felt more than that.

"You're leaving?" she'd said, her face going pale as she looked up from the dishes she was washing.

"Got to. They're waiting."

"I know, but—" she picked up a towel and dried her hands as she came toward him "—I thought... When will you be back?"

"Dunno." He shrugged and gave her his best rakish grin. "You know us rodeo cowboys. Always goin' down the road. Never stayin' in one place more than a night or two."

"You stayed here two weeks." She was looking like a wounded doe.

"'Cause I was hurt."

"And now you're well." He heard a faint bitterness in her voice as she turned away to stare out the window.

He dropped the duffel bag and saddle and jammed his hands into his pockets. "Now I'm well," he agreed. "Thanks to you," he added gently, wishing she would smile.

She didn't. Her fingers knotted in front of her.

He yanked a hand out of his pocket and touched her arm. She stiffened.

"Come on, Tess. Don't be like this. You knew I was goin'."

"Did I?" He heard the ache in her voice and tried to ignore it.

"Course you did. It's what I do, for Lord's sake. I got to. I never said I'd stay!"

She didn't look at him, didn't speak.

Outside Taggart yelled, "Hey, Noah, hurry it up!"

"See? I gotta..." He stared at her helplessly.

She shook him off. "Fine. Go." Noah saw a tear slip down her cheek, then another. She swiped them angrily away, then hugged her arms against her breasts. "They're waiting for you."

Damn it, he hated it when women cried! And over him! He couldn't believe it. He gripped her arm again, pulling her around, trying to make her face him. "Look, Tess. I didn't mean for this to happen. You know that. I never said...I never made any promises, did I? Did I?"

She looked at him then. It didn't help.

"I didn't," he reiterated desperately. "I can't. I got nothing to give you."

"Love."

Love? It couldn't be so simple. What about jobs? Money? Hopes? Dreams?

His hesitation was enough. Tess jerked out of his grasp and spun away from him. "Go on. Go away!"

But her misery was so clear he couldn't seem to move. "I can't... I need..."

"Well, I don't!" She jerked the door open and stood waiting, glaring at him. "I said go on!"

Noah's fingers clenched. His lips pressed into a tight line. "Fine," he said heavily after a moment. "I'm going." He yanked up the saddle and duffel bag and started past her. She was too close, too tempting. He leaned toward her and brushed a hard kiss across her lips, then turned once more on the top step. "I'll call you."

"No."

"I'll call you," he said firmly.

But he almost hadn't.

"Don't," Taggart had counseled. "It isn't fair. You don't want to keep her danglin', do you?"

A part of Noah did want to. The selfish part. The part that woke up several times a night after he'd left her, missing her. Longing for her laugh, for her smile, for the gentle way she touched him. The part that seemed always to be looking for her sweet, generous nature in every girl who flirted with him or teased him or knocked on his motel-room door.

But none of them was Tess. And Tess was the only one he hankered after. The only one he lay awake at night and wished for.

But Taggart was right. What could he offer her, besides the occasional night when he was passing through?

There was no point even thinking about it. Finally, in mid-September, he called her to tell her so.

"Noah?" she'd said when she heard his voice. "Oh, Noah!"

She sounded so pathetically happy to get his call, he'd felt like a heel for dragging it out this long. "Hi, Tess." He made himself sound cheerful, upbeat.

"Are you in town?"

"I'm in California. I been runnin' all over. You know what it's like."

"I guess," she said vaguely. "When are you coming?"

He took a deep breath. "I'm not."

"Not? At all?" Her voice was suddenly faint, as if he'd knocked the wind right out of her. All the eagerness he'd heard just moments before was gone.

He wanted desperately to put it back. He didn't dare. "Not at all," he said firmly. "I just... just didn't want to leave you wondering what had happened to me." He paused. "And I said I'd call so... here I am."

Over the wires he heard the long-distance hum. "Yes, well, thank you," she said finally, after so long a time he thought she might not still be there. She sounded very polite now. Very formal. "It was kind of you to let me know."

Kind? Not hardly. He wished he could think of something else to say, something that would make her feel better, make her know that this was for her own good, that she deserved a far better man than him. Somehow he didn't think she'd appreciate a testimonial.

"You... been all right?" he asked her at last.

"Fine," she said. "Just fine."

"Good. Good." He hesitated. "I, uh, gotta run. I'll see—" he paused awkwardly "—no, I guess I won't."

And he hadn't.

Until Tuesday.

* * *

"He's been asking for you," Nita told Tess two days later when she came back from her day off.

Tess didn't reply at once. She hung up her coat and shook the snowflakes from her hair, doing her best to feign indifference, though her heart had been beating faster for the past five days. She'd been desperate for a day off to regain her equilibrium, hoping it would be enough. It wasn't. Damn Noah Tanner for being able to affect her this way still. "Who's been asking?" she said finally, though she was sure she knew.

"The dark-haired cowboy with the to-die-for blue eyes. He's cuter than Derek, I'll give you that. Surely you've noticed."

"I can't say that I have," Tess lied. "How's Mrs. Forrest this morning?"

"Mrs. Forrest went home yesterday. Here. Breakfast just came up. Why don't you take around the trays. And—" Nita winked "—while you're at it, check out those eyes."

Tess grumbled, but took the cart full of trays. She knew all too well the mesmerizing power of Noah Tanner's blue eyes. She prayed they'd be closed—that he'd be asleep.

He wasn't.

"Hey, sunshine." He was still lying down, but he smiled at her when she appeared.

"Noah." She set his tray on the table.

"I figured maybe you were avoiding me, but Nita said you had the day off. I wanted to ask you, what's the debt of gratitude for?"

Oh, hell. He would remember that. "I was just glad you called that day," she said at last. "Put an end to it."

He looked at her closely. "I didn't want to give you false hopes."

"I appreciate it," she said dryly. At the time it had crushed her. When she had more perspective, she'd come to see he was right. She didn't want a man who didn't love her, who wouldn't be there for her.

"Figured you'd find a lot better man than me. Did you?"

Almost at the door, she turned to look at him. "Did I what?"

His blue eyes were boring into her. "Find a better man? Marry him?"

She hesitated. "I'm not married," she said at last.

Why the hell not?

If there was ever a woman who ought to be married, it was Tess Montgomery. Even a dyed-in-the-wool drifter— *especially* a dyed-in-the-wool drifter—like Noah Tanner could see that.

She was a nester, right down to her toes. Even in the slapped-together one-bedroom apartment where she'd been living, a place with as much inherent personality as a chicken coop, Tess Montgomery had created a home. And she'd wanted kids. She'd said so.

The men in Wyoming must be fools, Noah thought. Or eunuchs.

Or—*hadn't she married because of him?*

He shouldn't dare to think any such thing. And he didn't. Not really. Even he wasn't that cocky.

But Noah couldn't suppress a tiny grin as, deep down, some little-bitty part of him couldn't help wondering if it was so.

Taggart wasn't a fool. Or a eunuch.

And even though he was even more bruised and battered looking than Noah, not to mention tied to the bed with his right leg suspended in traction, when Noah finally got to

visit his buddy, he found himself wishing Taggart wasn't
quite so attractive to the opposite sex.

Or to Tess. Because he was, if that heart-stopping smile
she was wearing when she came into Taggart's room was
anything to go by.

"Good morning," she said in a cheerful tone Noah never
heard when she came into his room.

And then she saw Noah sitting by the window and her
smiled faded.

Taggart, who'd been complaining about hospitals and
doctors and food and how he couldn't wait to get out of
here, took one look at Tess and his face lit up. "Hey, my
favorite nurse!" He tried to shove himself up farther in the
bed.

Favorite nurse? What the hell did that mean?

"Don't do that," Tess said sharply to Taggart. "You'll
hurt yourself. Here. Let me help you." She put an arm
around his shoulders and settled him back against the pillows, then raised the head of the bed a foot or so. "How's
that?"

"Great." Taggart gave her another grin and blew her a
kiss. "You're my angel, aren't you, Tessie?"

Tessie? Noah's jaw clamped shut.

"This pretty lady is the only thing that makes bein' here
tolerable," Taggart said. "She takes good care of me, don't
you?"

"I try," Tess said with a demure smile. "What do you
need?"

"You got any more of that orange juice?"

"Of course." And she vanished to get some.

"Wish they were all that sweet," Taggart said to Noah
after she'd brought them each a glass, given Taggart a smile,
Noah a nod, and left again.

"She's not that sweet to me," Noah grumbled.

Taggart lifted an eyebrow. "I thought all the girls fell at your feet."

"Not Tess. Not this time, anyhow."

"This time?"

"I was here before, remember? The time I got concussed ridin' Maverick's Dream."

Taggart blinked, then stared. "Tess is *her?* The one you..."

Noah gave a single affirmative jerk of his head. Then he reached over and picked up a copy of the football magazine on Taggart's bedside table, opening it and at least pretending to read.

"So are you still interested?" Taggart asked. He wasn't talking about football.

Noah kept his eyes on the magazine. "She was a nice girl."

"Still is."

Noah looked up and gave his friend a hard look. "Not one to be fooling around with," he said gruffly. "She deserves better."

Taggart grinned. "You are still interested."

"I'm not dead!"

"And thank God for that." Taggart smiled, then said reflectively, "When I came around, I didn't know what had happened to you."

"I saw you unconscious. I thought you'd bought the ranch. You looked like it," Noah answered, grateful for the change in subject.

"Bruised my pretty face," Taggart agreed. He grimaced and glanced at his leg. "And did this." They both stared in silent contemplation at the strapped-up, plaster-cast appendage.

"Good thing you aren't ridin' this week," Noah said. "You might've had to turn him out."

Taggart smiled, but the smile didn't quite reach his eyes. "Might've," he agreed. "My folks are on their way down with Becky. I didn't want 'em to bring her, told 'em it'd scare her, seein' me like this. But they said she'd be scared worse if they didn't."

Noah hadn't thought about that, about what it meant to have someone depending on you to be well, to bring home the bacon. He'd called Tanner when he'd become coherent, long enough to tell his brother he'd been in a little accident and that he might not be there for a while. But Tanner had his own life, his own worries—a wife, three kids, a struggling ranch. He wasn't depending on Noah.

No one was.

And a good thing, too, he thought now.

"You'll be glad to see her," he said with as much cheerful determination as he could muster.

"Yeah." Taggart looked away and blinked rapidly. "I missed her damned Christmas program, though," he said roughly.

"She understands."

"I should've been there."

"We tried."

Taggart was staring out the window. "I'm gonna quit riding."

"*What?*" It was a good thing he was sitting down, Noah thought, or he'd have fallen right over.

"I'm retirin'. Stayin' home." Taggart spelled it out for him.

"You're just saying that 'cause you're hurt. When you feel better, you'll change your mind."

Taggart shook his head. "No. I won't."

"You can't quit," Noah said urgently. "What would you do? What *can* you do?" Riding bulls wasn't a stepping stone to a lot of other careers any more than riding broncs was.

"I'll think of something."

"You can't. You—"

"Shut up," Taggart said, as his gaze flicked suddenly from the window to a movement in the doorway. He straightened up against the pillows and pasted a smile on his face. "They're here."

And before Noah could ease his still-stiff body around, Taggart's parents appeared at his side, his gray-haired, tanned father smiling nervously, his thin, usually cheerful mother looking desperate as she focused on her son. A second later a small body brushed against Noah's arm. He turned his head to see Becky. He'd never seen Taggart's daughter less than irrepressible, but now she looked haunted, her eyes wide with worry as she stared at the man in the bed.

"D-Daddy?"

Taggart held out a hand to her. "It's okay, Beck. *I'm* okay."

For a moment she seemed to doubt him. But when he beckoned again, she flew at him, crying, scrabbling up onto the bed. Grimacing with pain and ignoring it at the same time, Taggart hauled his daughter up into his arms and hugged her tight.

"Oh, dear!"

Tess stood in the doorway, looking momentarily horrified at Becky's assault on the bed. Noah thought she was going to sweep the little girl out of Taggart's arms. Instead she scooped her up, shifted her around and settled her down gently once more so that Taggart could still hold her but she wouldn't hurt his leg.

"There." Tess's hand brushed lightly over the child's fair hair. "Better?" she asked gently.

Becky hugged her father, reached up and traced his bruised cheek lightly, then glanced once at Tess and nodded shyly. And Noah saw both of Taggart's parents begin to breathe again. Gaye, his mother, even smiled as she moved toward the bed to take his hand and drop a kiss on his hair.

Will Jones didn't move, but his smile broadened. "Thank God, son," he said, and Noah heard the emotion in his voice.

Watching them, Noah felt an ache inside that had nothing to do with his injuries. He looked away. "I'll see you around," he said as he got up.

At his words, Taggart's parents seemed to notice him all at once. "Oh, Noah!" Gaye said now. "Are you all right?"

"I'm fine," he said, edging toward the door.

"You poor thing. You look worse than Taggart."

Noah shook his head and kept moving.

"You don't have to go," Gaye protested.

"You visit with Taggart. That's what you came for."

"But—"

Tess stepped between them. "He really does need to rest," she said to Taggart's mother. "He's been up far too long." And she stayed between them until Noah was out of the room.

"Thanks."

She hesitated. "Don't you like them?"

"Of course I like them. They're Taggart's parents."

"Then why...?"

Noah cast around for words to express feelings he didn't completely understand himself. "They aren't *my* parents," he said finally, after a moment.

She must have remembered that his parents were dead, for the smile she gave him was one of gentle sadness. "Come on," she said. "Let's get you back to bed."

* * *

It wasn't much. Just the barest hint of empathy. But even so, it was the only real hint he'd had so far that she still felt something for him.

He embroidered on it for hours. Days. He couldn't help himself. He was going stir-crazy, lying around the damned hospital. The hour he spent in physical therapy every day left him exhausted and shaking, but for the most part, hour by hour he felt stronger, healthier and as if the walls were closing in on him. The only way out was in his mind.

And the only thing on his mind was Tess.

"How come you haven't married?" he asked her one morning.

She was taking his blood pressure, but from the sudden color in her face, it was hers that ought to be checked. "None of your business."

"It could be."

"No." She brushed a lock of hair away from her face as she moved away.

He shoved himself up in the bed. "I'm not saying it is," Noah said conversationally. "I'm only sayin' it might be. If, for example, you were carryin' a torch for me."

"Carry a torch for you? Think again, cowboy!"

Noah grinned, then sobered. "It was good, Tess," he said quietly.

She was writing something on his chart. She didn't look up.

"You were good. Too good for me. You still singin' in the choir at church?" He remembered how amazed he'd been when she'd popped out of bed after the Saturday night they'd spent loving. He'd been even more amazed when she'd told him where she was going.

People he knew believed in God, all right. Some of them even went to church. But no one he knew went so far as to sing in a choir. He'd gone along and listened, enthralled at the pure, sweet sound of Tess's soprano solo. Later, when they'd curled together in bed, she'd sung once more, softly and sweetly, just for him. "Do you?" he persisted when she kept writing.

"Yes."

"Gonna sing at Christmas?"

She nodded.

"You're staying in Laramie then? Not goin' home?"

"This is my home." He knew her parents were dead, too, but he remembered she had a sister somewhere in Wyoming. "My family's here now," she told him. She finished making notes on his chart and started toward the door.

"Tess?"

She turned.

"Sing to me."

She fled.

Call it arrogance.

Call it cockiness.

It was, sure enough.

Call it wrong-headed and selfish. It was that, too. And the product of too much time spent wishful thinking. But Noah couldn't help it. He was convinced she still cared.

She might act calm and cool and professional. She might deny that he mattered to her at all. But if he didn't, why did she avoid him, ignore him, then blush like a schoolgirl when he reminded her of intimacies they'd shared?

She cared. And he wanted her to admit it. To him. To herself.

That was probably why he kissed her.

If there was any rational reason for it at all.

He sure to goodness didn't plan it. He'd been sitting there, staring at the same damn four walls all the next morning, contemplating how he could get the doc to release him and how he was then going to get to Tanner and Maggie's when he did, when Tess came to take him to physical therapy.

She was brisk and bossy, and she acted like he meant no more to her than old man Hardesty across the hall.

So he kissed her.

To make her angry? Probably. To make her respond? Definitely.

She was right there, holding him up, helping him move from the bed to the wheelchair. So close. So impersonal.

And so he kissed her.

It was a hungry kiss. A demanding kiss. A kiss that sought to resurrect memories that eight years had been doing their best to erase. And the moment that his lips touched hers, the eight years vanished just like that. It might have been yesterday. Hell, it felt like yesterday.

He'd kissed a lot of women in the past eight years. None of them kissed with the same sweet hunger as Tess Montgomery.

Until at least, she realized that she was kissing him back. Then she jerked away, her face scarlet, her breasts heaving beneath her starched white uniform. She gave him a shove that sent him flat on the bed.

"Damn you, Noah Tanner!" She spun around and fled from the room.

Noah, ribs aching, knee throbbing, shoulder pounding, lay back and touched his lips and grinned.

Two

"What do you mean, I can't come for Christmas?"

Robert Tanner rubbed the back of his neck and looked around the tiny hospital room as if he wished he were somewhere else—anywhere else. Noah knew how he felt. He felt that way himself—and the news his brother had just imparted didn't help matters a bit.

"They want you here," Tanner said helplessly.

Noah had been surprised and delighted when his older brother had walked into his room ten minutes earlier. Then, seeing some gaily wrapped Christmas packages, he'd been curious. Now he was just plain mad.

"But Taggart left. He left today!" Noah argued.

With Becky and his parents hovering in the background, Taggart had crutched his way in to say goodbye less than two hours ago. He'd even grinned and said, "Hey, it won't be long for you. Come on up to Montana when you can."

And now Tanner was telling Noah he wasn't going any-where!

"Why can't I?" he demanded.

"Physical therapy on the knee, apparently. If you'd had surgery, they might've let you come. Given you a chance to mend a bit before they put you through the torture. But since you didn't..." Tanner didn't need to finish the sentence. "Three times a week for now, the doc said. And we can't get you here from there—it's a good seven hours one way. You know that."

"So I'm supposed to stay in the hospital?"

"They didn't say that," Tanner said in the same tone he used to soothe jittery horses. "You can leave tomorrow or the day after. Soon as you get the all clear on the lung."

Noah muttered under his breath and poked at the macaroni and cheese on his lunch tray. "Hell."

Tanner crushed his hat brim with his fingers. "Oh, I don't know. You might find it restful. A damn sight more restful than the ranch is gonna be. Wall-to-wall rug rats at our place." He tried to sound disgruntled, but didn't manage it.

"I was looking forward to it," Noah said gruffly. It was the truth. Christmas had come to seem a lot more like Christmas since Jared was born. Even when he was only a few months old, Jared had made Christmas special. Last year, when he was toddling around, shredding wrapping paper and gumming the wise men in the hearthside manger, his innocent, wide-eyed joy had made it even more so. And now that Tanner and Maggie had eleven-month-old Seth and Nick, and Luke and Jill had eight-month-old Keith, Noah thought things would be even better.

Probably they still would be. Without him.

"Hell," he said again.

"We'll miss you," Tanner offered lamely. "We're just grateful you're alive," he added, and Noah saw a shudder run through his brother as he contemplated what could have happened. "You're damn lucky."

He didn't feel especially lucky. He still hurt. He hadn't even begun to let himself think about when he might be able to go down the road again. And now he couldn't even go to Tanner's for Christmas. Neither of them spoke for a long moment. It wasn't the holiday they'd counted on. It could have been much better.

It could have been much worse.

"I'm glad you came," Noah said at last, mustering all the good cheer he could.

"I'd have come first thing, but Jared had the flu and the twins were cuttin' teeth, and I couldn't leave Maggie to cope with all of it."

"No. I knew you'd come if you could. You always do."

If something ever needed to be done, Tanner did it. He had been the responsible brother from the very start—taking care, taking charge—far different from Noah and Luke, who were always ready to move on and never look around— or back.

Now Tanner reached over to the bedside table and picked up the gold buckle Noah had won at the NFR. He weighed it in his hand, then looked at his brother. "I never did this."

"I may never do it again."

"Don't matter. You got nothin' left to prove. Took some grit. And I reckon gettin' healed will take some more grit."

"Taggart says he's quitting." Noah still couldn't quite believe it.

"I'm not surprised."

Noah blinked. "How come? He's got grit, too. A hell of a lot of it. Had to have, takin' care of Becky."

"Exactly. Kids have a way of makin' you look at the long haul. And makin' you want to stick around."

"I wouldn't know."

Tanner smiled. "One day you will."

"Not likely," Noah said gruffly. "I'm not exactly dad material."

There was a sound from the doorway, like an indrawn breath, and he glanced up to see Tess.

It was the first he'd seen of her since he'd kissed her. She looked stricken and started to turn away.

"It's okay if you want the lunch tray," he called after her. He wanted to talk to her, but not now. Not in front of Tanner.

She turned. "No. Not if you're not finished," she said stiffly.

"I'm finished," he said. "Come meet my brother."

Tess hesitated.

Noah beckoned to her. "He looks mean, but he doesn't bite." He knew she was a damn sight more wary of him than of his brother, but after another moment, she came slowly into the room.

"This is Tann—I mean, Robert. The nicest one of us. This," he told Tanner, "is Tess."

There must have been something in his tone that made Tanner take a closer look. Since his marriage, Tanner had never noticed any woman other than Maggie, but he was definitely checking out Tess now.

She smiled a little self-consciously, then held out her hand. "I'm glad one of you is nice."

"You can count on it." Tanner flicked a glance at Noah. "Been givin' you trouble, has he? I'm not surprised. You just got to ignore him."

"I'm doing my best."

"Don't let him get to you," Tanner went on.

"I won't."

They didn't have to talk about him as if he wasn't even there. Goaded, Noah said, "I already did."

Tess's cheeks turned a faint pink, but she ignored him and reached for his tray.

"I kissed her."

Her faintly flushed cheeks turned crimson. She snatched his tray off the table and made for the door.

"And she kissed me back. Didn't you, Tess?" he called.

But Tess had disappeared, shoving the clattering meal cart down the hall like she was qualifying for the Indy 500.

Tanner watched her go, then turned back to regard his brother speculatively. "I think you're askin' for trouble."

"Already got it."

"Because you kissed her?"

Noah shrugged. "There's a little more to it than that."

"Figured there might be." Tanner waited in case Noah decided to enlighten him.

Noah ran his tongue over his lips. "Years back we—well, we..." *We what? Slept together? Made love? Had an affair?*

How did you describe what had gone on between them for those two brief weeks? Noah plucked irritably at the blanket. "It's a hell of a mess."

"Seems like."

"Any brotherly advice?"

Tanner's eyes widened at the unlikely question. "Me? Sorry. I don't reckon the Tanner brothers are all that gifted when it comes to dealin' with women."

"Ain't that the truth?"

Tanner stood staring at the door, lost in thought. "She's a mighty pretty lady, though." A slow smile spread across his face and he looked at his brother. "If you play your cards right, I reckon you just might find yourself a place to stay for Christmas."

Noah didn't think all the tricks in the book would get him that.

* * *

He was gone. At last.

Discharged at 10:40 this morning, while she hid in the nurses' lounge, cowering behind a cup of decaf and a Danish and letting Nita see him into the wheelchair and out the door.

So she was a chicken. Nobody ever said she had to be brave. She simply had to survive.

And she would. Now.

She hadn't been so sure after that kiss. The kiss had devastated her.

Damn Noah Tanner, anyway. How dared he catch her off guard like that? How dared he kiss her as if he had every right?

How dared she kiss him back?

Because God knew—and she knew—that she had. She had, for a few moments, opened to him like a parched flower that, after eight long years in the desert, at last was given rain. His kiss had come so unexpectedly, so astonishingly, that she hadn't thought; she had only reacted.

And the worst thing was it had felt so terribly, terribly right. As if all the years and all the pain had fallen away, leaving only the man.

She'd been telling herself that the only reason Noah had mattered so much was because he was the first man who'd taken the time to get behind the facade to the real Tess Montgomery. The first man to whom she'd uncovered her inner self.

A country girl who had grown up rambling the hills by herself, Tess had never been given to easy conversation or the best of social graces. She was quiet and self-contained, more given to spending time with animals than people. Not that she didn't like people; she did. She just didn't have a lot of experience with them.

Nursing had appealed to her from the time she was small. "Tessie's got a healin' touch," her father always used to say. And it was true. She could take a sick calf and make it well again. The rabbits they kept in the shed near the house died for her sister but thrived for her. And when her mother had suffered from cancer throughout most of Tess's teenage years, it was her ministrations that made Susannah Montgomery relax and smile.

Tess knew even before her mother died that nursing was what she would do, if the money was there for school. It almost wasn't. But she'd got through the first year and a half with her father's help before his horse stumbled in a prairie-dog hole and he was thrown and killed. That had happened a little more than a year before the summer she met Noah. She was on her own then, living in a tiny apartment not far from the campus, working two jobs to afford her last year of nurse's training. Her older sister, Nancy, had married and moved to Omaha the previous spring. Tess had a few friends at work and at school, but little time to go out with them. Mostly she was alone.

She didn't realize how alone, or how much she longed for someone to share things with, until that dark-haired, blue-eyed bronc rider charmed his way from his hospital bed into her life.

She'd never done anything like that before—taken a man home. Especially not to stay. She never would have dared take a man like Noah home with her if he was operating at full strength. But he wasn't. In fact, he seemed to need her.

Heaven knew she needed him.

She hadn't realized just how much. It could still make her cheeks warm and her insides lurch if she dwelt very long on how foolish and naive she'd been eight years ago. In a matter of only a few days, she'd shared everything with him— her life, her hopes, her fears, her dreams. Her body.

Even now she blushed at how eagerly she had shared the intimacies of the flesh with him. Noah Tanner knew more about her than anyone in the world.

When he'd left, a part of her had died.

It was her own fault, of course. She knew that. He'd made no promises. He'd been sweet, gentle, caring. He'd been by turns whimsical, serious and funny. He'd been her friend, her confidant, her lover. But he'd never intended it to be permanent.

She'd only prayed he would.

She should have known better. Noah Tanner was a rodeo cowboy. A man who made his living going from place to place. A man whose dreams lay just over the next hill. He couldn't stay. It wasn't who he was.

Still, fool that she was, she'd hoped. Even after the battered red pickup had come and borne him away. After all, hadn't he said he'd call? Didn't that mean something?

When a month passed, and then another, she'd begun to suspect it didn't. Even as she found things she desperately needed to share with him, she began to think she never could.

And then one bright September day, the phone rang.

She'd known his voice at once. They'd never talked on the phone, but she hadn't a doubt from the first tentative, slightly gruff, "Tess?" that it was him. She hadn't been able to contain her joy. Just as, seconds later, when he told her he wasn't coming back—ever—she hadn't been able to disguise her pain.

More foolishness.

But she'd made up her mind that she wasn't going to be a fool any longer. She was going to grow up, become the woman she'd always wanted to become.

And for all intents and purposes, she had.

Until early last Monday morning, when Noah Tanner kissed her again.

She'd steered clear, stonewalled, resisted. And she'd almost made it.

And then, without warning, he'd given her a kiss, and her resolutions had gone up in flames. Her indifference had crumbled at her feet. Like it or not, she'd turned into the same besotted idiot she'd been all those years before.

Why?

Because no one had ever taken his place.

Not really. Not completely. Oh, there had been a few brief encounters. With Mark, the respiratory therapist. With Steven, the CPA. With Jon and Jeff and Warren, with whom she'd managed two dates apiece. But all the men in the last eight years of her life she could count on the fingers of one hand. And not one of them had really known her.

Not the way Noah had known her.

Nita was right. It was time she got a man in her life.

Noah was an expert on motels. He appreciated even heat, cable television, spotless sheets and personal coffee makers. He was glad to be near the ice machine, so he had only a few feet to walk to replenish the bags of ice he was still putting on his knee.

But all the warm air, ice bags, coffee and holiday television specials in the world didn't do the trick.

It was Christmas, damn it. He wanted to be where the kids would be romping and shouting, the logs would be crackling in the fireplace, where Christmas carols would be playing in the background and the smells of gingerbread and cinnamon would be teasing his every breath.

He didn't want absolute silence, even if it meant excellent soundproofing. He didn't want to smell disinfectant, no matter how clean it meant the bathroom was.

He wanted to go home.

He shoved himself up off the bed and hobbled to the window, opened the drapes and stared out into the heavy snowfall. If he were ten years younger, he'd grab his gear and head for the interstate, determined to hitch a ride and say the hell with physical therapy. But he wasn't.

He was almost thirty-four. He felt more like sixty. God knew he had more miles on him than most sixty-year-olds. And if God didn't know it, his bones, muscles and sinews did. If he wanted to ride broncs again he had to stay and do his three-times-a-week therapy. There was no choice.

Taggart wasn't riding again, he reminded himself. Yeah, but Taggart had a reason not to, and parents who would let him take his time finding his feet again.

Noah didn't. He had brothers, sure, but he didn't want to impose on them. If worse came to worst, he supposed he could cowboy for Tanner for a while. He might even be able to go out to California and visit Luke and Jill, or head up to the range camp where Luke had holed up until Jill had flushed him out last year. But he couldn't stay there like his brother had.

He wouldn't last more than a week. Tanner and Luke were loners—strong, silent, solitary men. Noah needed people, excitement, challenge, not what he would get at the cabin—unrelenting solitude and the ongoing opportunity to face the flat, bleak nothing that was his future.

His future.

What future?

He looked at his pale face in the motel-room mirror. "And a very merry Christmas to you."

He lasted two days.

Two days of staring at four beige walls, one beige carpet, a beige-and-gray bedspread and reruns of every tear-jerking seasonal movie ever made. He called Tanner twice. The first evening he tried his best to sound both stoic and upbeat as he talked to his sister-in-law Maggie, too. The following night he spoke with Luke and Jill, as well. He hoped that just listening to them all—Tanner, Maggie, Luke, Jill and even Jared—would be enough or that it would make him glad he wasn't there.

By the time he hung up, he felt more lonely and bereft than ever. He got out the phone book and looked up Tess.

He didn't exactly intend to call her. He just wanted the number—to hang on to—whatever sense that made.

But then, as he watched the rest of *Miracle on 34th Street*, he found himself dialing her number before he stopped to think.

He got an answering machine.

"Hi," Tess's soft voice said, "Hope you're having a merry. Leave a message and we'll get back to you." There was none of the drill sergeant that he'd heard when she talked to him at the hospital. This was the warm Tess, the welcoming Tess. The Tess he remembered all too well. The machine beeped, waiting.

Noah hung up.

She was at work, of course. Or was she? Last week she'd had this day off. He sat hunched on the side of the bed, wondering where she was. Christmas shopping? Choir practice? *Out with another man?*

That idea stung. He slumped back against the headboard of the bed and contemplated his cool, beige surroundings. He remembered Tess's tiny apartment, painted a cozy buttercup yellow. Her furniture had been vintage garage sale, but she'd had a pile of colorful pillows on the sofa and cheerful travel posters on the wall. Her bedroom had been painted a soft blue with a double bed that sagged in the middle where they had rolled together every night.

They hadn't cared. They'd touched. Kissed. Loved.

Remembering, Noah shut his eyes and groaned.

He grabbed the remote control and clicked on the television, surfing through the channels, finding nothing to distract him. In his mind her soft voice played over and over again. *Hope you're having a merry.*

Yeah, he thought. *Right.*

He had to be at the hospital at one for physical therapy. The foot of snow that had fallen two days ago had been plowed aside, but as his taxi pulled up in front of the hospital, snow began to fall again.

He looked for her at the hospital. He saw Nita. She waved to him. He waved back, then crutched toward the physical-therapy room. He thought Tess might come in while he was waiting or while he was sweating and groaning through the weights and the bike and the stretching. He hoped she might come in after. He never saw her once.

On his way out, he stopped for a cup of coffee in the cafeteria, telling himself he needed the liquid refreshment. What he needed was a glimpse of Tess.

One of the other nurses from the orthopedic department smiled at him. Nita waved to him again as he hobbled back toward the lobby.

It was snowing harder now. The streets were thick with it as the cab took him back to his beige prison. He tried to steel himself to go in, but when the cab pulled up in front of the motel, he couldn't do it.

"Wait for me," he said.

He got his gear and checked out.

He didn't expect Tess to welcome him with open arms. He knew better. But there had been something between them once—something he'd walked away from.

He wasn't asking for that back.

He was asking for a little friendship, a little understanding, a home just until Christmas was over. A few days. No more. Then he'd go back to the motel.

Then he could face the beige.

Her address wasn't the same as before. He didn't know what to expect this time, but was pleased to find that she lived on a street fairly near the university. It was in a neighborhood with trees and older homes and even the occasional picket fence, including one in front of hers. Exactly the sort of place he'd imagined her in.

Her particular house was a steep-roofed, white framed two-story with a huge fir tree in the front yard. The house looked solid and substantial and entirely too big and settled for one person. He wondered suddenly if she lived alone. She'd said her family was here now. He knew her parents were dead. Perhaps her sister and family had moved to Laramie? Would they welcome a stranger for Christmas?

Noah peered out the window, having second thoughts. Especially when he spotted a young girl in the front yard, rolling a ball to make a snowman. She had hair the color of Tess's and her cheeks were flushed from the cold. A niece? Probably. So the sister did live here.

"This *is* the right address?" the cab driver asked when Noah made no move to get out.

"Yeah. Yeah, I guess it is." He hesitated still, then thought about the beige walls again. Perhaps it would be better with her sister's family there; she'd be less likely to throw him out.

He paid the driver and got out of the cab, then stood holding his duffel bag in one hand and leaning on his crutches.

The girl in the yard was watching him. Close up, she looked even more like Tess. Beneath the wind flush on her cheeks, he could see Tess's freckles. Her nose was Tess's, too. Her hair was long and dark, just like Tess's had been when he'd first known her. Only her eyes were different. Tess's were a soft jade green. This girl's were a deep, dark blue. She didn't take them off him for a second.

"I'm looking for Tess Montgomery," he said finally. "Is she home?"

The girl shook her dark head. "Not yet," she said. "She'll . . . be home by three-thirty."

"Do you mind if I wait?"

She ran her tongue across her lips. "No," she said faintly. "You can wait," she said with a little more enthusiasm.

Noah slowly made his way through the snow and opened the gate. Seeing his awkwardness, she took his bag and set it on the front porch. He smiled. An ally.

She turned back to look at him again as he shut the gate, her scrutiny so intense it was a little unnerving.

"Nice snowman," he said.

"Thanks."

"I'd help but I'm . . . sort of laid up."

"Yes."

"I'm Noah Tanner," he said finally, realizing she had no idea.

"I know."

"You do?" Amazing. How many girls her age knew a world-champion bronc rider when they saw one? "Did Tess tell you about me?"

She nodded solemnly.

He grinned, pleased as punch. "You really know who I am?"

"You're my father," she said.

Three

———

He hadn't heard her right.

He *couldn't* have heard her right. "What did you say?"

"I said you're my... father." There was a faint hesitation, but no real question even now. He tightened his grip on the crutches.

"Your father?" How could he make it a question when she was looking at him with such wide-eyed sincerity. *How could he not?*

"I'm Susannah."

He couldn't even seem to get his tongue around her name. *"Susannah!"* They both turned as Tess came running down the sidewalk, a panic-stricken look on her face.

Susannah beamed. "Mom! Look! Look who's here!"

Tess reached the gate and grabbed the pickets with both hands. Her eyes flicked from the beaming child to Noah. They stayed fastened on him. "What are you doing here?"

"Meeting my daughter?" He twisted the word. He couldn't help it.

There was a certain bitter irony to the whole situation that he was sure he would appreciate—given, perhaps, a hundred years. Right now he was having trouble believing it—believing her.

How could she not have told him he had a daughter, for God's sake?

Tess fumbled with the latch, then got it open. She crossed the yard to put her arm around Susannah. "Go put on the milk and we'll have some cocoa."

"But—"

"Go on. Now."

She sounded like a stern mother. Hell, Noah realized, she *was* a stern mother.

"But I want—" Susannah pleaded. When she got a look even sterner than the voice, she turned reluctantly and headed toward the door.

She'd barely gone ten feet when Tess rounded on Noah. "I don't know why you're here," she said in a furious undertone, "but I want you to leave. Now."

"No."

"You have no business here!"

"Apparently I have a daughter here."

She swallowed. "So?"

"So?" He positively gaped at her. "I find that out and you expect me to hop back in a cab and go away?"

"Yes." It was a hiss.

He shook his head. Slowly. Adamantly. "No."

"Damn it, Noah—"

"Damn it, Tess," he said mildly. "I'm not leaving. Unless," he added, "you want to tell me she's wrong. Is she?"

Tess hesitated, as if she'd love to say yes, then sighed. "No. She's not. But it doesn't matter," she said, meeting his gaze defiantly.

"What the hell do you mean, it doesn't matter?"

"She doesn't need you. She's done just fine for almost eight years without you. She can keep doing fine without you."

"Why should she?"

"What?" Tess looked at him, aghast.

Noah stuck his chin out. "Why should she do without me now that I know about her?" He wasn't exactly sure what he was proposing. He just knew he had less reason than ever to walk away.

Tess's mouth opened and closed. "Because," she said finally, in the same fierce undertone, "our lives are fine the way they are. We don't need you coming in and disrupting things. Invading our lives and then, whenever it suits you, disappearing again."

"You think that's what I'll do?"

"It's what you did." And with that she turned her back and started for the door. "Go away, Noah," she said over her shoulder. "I don't want you here."

"I do." Susannah's clear childish voice rang out in the stillness. Both of them jerked around to see her standing in the doorway, watching them. "I want him," she said to her mother. "I asked for him."

He could see them silhouetted in the living-room window, mother and daughter—Tess with her shoulders hunched, Susannah, chin lifted. Their mouths were moving. Noah would have given his championship buckle to know what they were saying. Tess had made him wait outside.

"Stay here," she'd commanded as she moved to follow her daughter into the house. Then she'd turned back. "Or don't. That would be even better."

Wild horses couldn't have dragged him away. He ought, he supposed, to be giving those wild horses a run for their money, trying to see how fast he could leave. But he was rooted to the spot. Stunned. Amazed.

Enchanted.

That pixie-faced child with the deep blue eyes was *his?*

Suddenly the silhouettes disappeared from view. The door opened. Tess came out onto the porch. She drew a deep breath, then came down the steps, her hands tucked into the pockets of her jacket. She planted her feet firmly, then looked up at him, resigned.

"Don't tell me I was on her Christmas list," Noah said lightly.

"Worse. She didn't ask Santa to bring you. She asked God. You are," Tess said, her mouth twisting in grim humor, "the answer to a prayer."

Tess supposed she was becoming a fatalist. How else could she accept the disaster that had just befallen her? How else could she simply open the door to her house and let Noah walk in, then act as if she didn't mind?

She minded. She just knew she couldn't do anything about it.

When her daughter had looked up at her with eyes so like Noah's and said in an aching voice, "Just once, Mom. I wanted him here just once. So I asked God. I thought if He made it happen, you wouldn't care," how on earth could she send him away?

So it was God's fault. There was no other explanation. Maybe God thought Susannah needed to see her father. Maybe God thought Noah needed to meet Susannah.

Tess knew hers was not to reason why. Hers was simply to cope.

Oh, but God, it's so hard, she said to the Almighty, lifting her eyes to the ceiling as she hopped out of her uniform slacks. *And so unfair. What are You thinking of?*

She didn't know if she'd get an answer. But if He'd heard Susannah, He could jolly well listen to her, too.

From the kitchen downstairs she could hear the faint murmur of Susannah's childish voice regaling Noah with heaven-knew-what indiscretion while they drank cocoa.

Tess hadn't known what else to do with him when he'd followed her into the house, so she'd made them cocoa, then hovered, hawklike, moving between the stove and the table where Noah and Susannah sat. Ready to swoop down on any untoward comment either of them made.

But then Susannah had said, "You're going to spill cocoa on your uniform, Mom," and she'd had no choice but to retreat to the bedroom and change into jeans and a sweater.

She was still hopping around on one foot when she heard them come up the stairs, then pass her room on their way to Susannah's.

Oh, heavens! Tess dragged her navy sweatshirt over her head and stuffed her feet into a pair of loafers. Then she hurried after them.

It was too late.

An hour ago he'd been in a beige motel room. Now he was in a whole new world. Noah felt as if he'd fallen down a rabbit hole or as if a phantom bronc had dropped him on his head.

Was he really sitting in Tess's kitchen drinking cocoa with his *daughter?*

Was she really telling him about her second-grade teacher? About the presents the Secret Santas in their classroom had exchanged? What the hell were Secret Santas, anyway? She acted like he ought to know. He pretended that he did.

He didn't know if he said anything coherent at all. If he didn't, Susannah didn't seem to mind.

When they finished their cocoa, she looked at him shyly and asked, "Want to see how I knew it was you?"

He nodded dumbly and followed her up the stairs, perusing as much of Tess's house as he could on the way.

It wasn't large, but it was cozy, with the same homey atmosphere he remembered from her apartment eight years ago. The living room had a raised-hearth fireplace and two six-over-six windows that looked out over the snowy front yard. The sofa was covered in a muted plaid, and there was a rather worn armchair near the fireplace, an afghan tossed over the back. On the other side of the hearth sat a pressed-oak rocker, similar to one he remembered his mother having. The kitchen was painted white with dark green trim and had a green-and-white latticework wallpaper. Tess had arranged copper teakettles of all shapes and sizes on a shelf near the ceiling. As they went up the stairs, Noah saw a row of pictures of Susannah, from infancy to, he presumed, second grade.

The house was warm and welcoming, and none of it was beige. Noah liked that a lot.

He caught a glimpse of what must be Tess's bedroom as Susannah led him past. "This is mine," she said, pushing open the last door. "See?" She pointed toward her bedside table.

On it were three pictures. The first was a recent one of Susannah and Tess in a boat in the summertime, laughing as they looked at each other. Next to it was a slightly faded snapshot in a silver frame of a much-younger Noah and Tess, their arms around each other. He was smiling at the camera and Tess was smiling at him. Noah's attention was arrested for a moment by the innocence he saw in her face— an innocence no longer there.

He turned away and looked at the third picture. It was a photo of him. A fairly recent one, taken at a rodeo. He was sweaty and grinning and being presented with a buckle.

"It's from when you won Cheyenne," Susannah said.

He blinked, startled. "Cheyenne? Last summer?" He braced himself on one crutch and picked up the small framed picture to study it. Then he looked at Susannah. "You were there?"

"I asked Mom if we could go. I wanted to see who you were."

"Why didn't you . . . " *introduce yourself?* he wanted to ask. *Tell me who you were?* He shook his head, dazed.

"Mom didn't think we should bother you," Susannah said in a small voice.

"Not bother me?" He stared at her.

She gave an awkward shrug. "She was afraid you might not want to know me and I'd get hurt."

"She thought I wouldn't want to know my own daughter?"

"She said . . . well, she didn't think I should get my hopes up. But she took me. We watched. You were *amazing.*" Her eyes seemed to almost light up at the memory.

"But if you were there, why didn't you come back by the chutes?"

"Mom said it wouldn't be fair, surprising you like that. We saw you in the midway after and I was going to, but…"

"But what?"

"You were throwing baseballs and you won a stuffed cat," she said almost desperately. "You gave it to this red haired lady with a little boy." She swallowed and looked up at him, her gaze haunted. "Is he...yours?"

"Susannah!" Tess appeared in the doorway. Her hair was tousled, her sweatshirt askew. Her gaze went worriedly from Noah to her daughter and back again.

Noah glanced at her, then at Susannah. He shook his head. "No, he's not," he said, realizing what she'd thought. "That was Jared. My nephew."

Tanner and Maggie had brought the boys down for the last weekend of the Cheyenne rodeo. They'd been there to see him win, and afterward they'd gone down the midway. Noah's luck had held even there. He'd won a toy for Jared and, later on, two more for the twins, though Tanner had already taken them back to the motel for a nap. He'd been in his element that day, playing with the boys, having a ball. And his own daughter had been just feet away!

"Jared's your cousin," he told her as the realization hit him.

Susannah sighed with something that could have been relief. "I thought he was yours."

"I don't have any kids." He paused. "Except you."

Tess drew in a sharp breath. He gave her a defiant look, and set the picture down firmly on the table, positioning it so Susannah could see it first thing in the morning.

"Do you mind?" Susannah asked timidly. "Having me, I mean."

A man could drown in the pure, clear innocence of those eyes. Blue eyes. *His* eyes. Noah shook his head slowly. "No, Susannah. I don't mind at all."

In Tess's dreams, the three of them had sat around the kitchen table like this—as a family—sharing the day's happenings, planning the evening's events.

Sometimes, when Susannah was little, she had even pretended that Noah was there to share in feeding their daughter her mashed banana and tiny, cut-up bits of chicken. Tess would glance up and imagine what it would be like to have him smile at her when Susannah did something silly. She would think how she would feel if he put his arm around her and gave her a kiss as, together, they shared their delight in their growing daughter.

And now, against all odds—and against not only her wishes, but her better judgment—here he was.

Tess looked away. "Eat your carrots, Susannah," she said sharply.

Susannah scowled. "You know I hate them," she said. "Do you hate them?" she asked Noah.

He did. Tess remembered that. But tonight he shook his head. "Nope," he said, and stabbed three, sticking them into his mouth and chewing manfully. Tess couldn't help smiling just a little.

"Love 'em. Good casserole, too," he said when he'd swallowed.

"We were going to have leftover roast," she told him bluntly. "But there wasn't enough for three."

"Sorry." But he didn't sound repentant. "I like this. I don't get a lot of casseroles on the road. It's fast food and junk mostly. Or steak."

"I like steak," Susannah told him. "But Mom says it's too expensive."

"We can go to the store later," Noah offered. "I'll buy groceries."

"I have enough money," Tess told him flatly. "I don't need your help."

"It's not help. It's sharing. I'm not here to freeload. I never did. You know that."

She did. Even nearly broke eight years ago, Noah had done his best to pay his own way. "You don't have to," she said now.

"We'll split it," he said. "How's that?"

Knowing that more argument would be futile, Tess muttered agreement into her applesauce.

"Steak," Susannah said happily. "And then we can get the tree." She turned to Noah. "You can help us pick it."

Tess wanted to say no. She couldn't, and she knew it. But, God, she protested silently, how much it hurt to have your prayers answered when you'd stopped praying!

Tess fixed her daughter with a hard stare. "We're not going anywhere, Susannah Marie, unless you eat every one of those carrots."

Grumbling, Susannah did. Then Tess washed the dishes and Noah dried them. She didn't want him to do that, either. She wanted him to leave her in peace. But if she said so, he'd go into the living room with Susannah, and she wanted that least of all! So when he asked for a dish towel, she gave him one and tried not to brush against his shirtsleeve with her elbow as she washed.

While they were doing the dishes, Susannah fed the cat. It was a long-haired, orange-marmalade tom that Susannah had found by the back door after a late-spring snowfall. They'd ignored it for several days, but it kept prowling around until finally Susannah prevailed upon Tess to let her feed it. Since then it had been part of their lives.

"What's its name?" Noah asked.

"Noah," Susannah replied, grinning.

Tess dropped a glass in the sink. "Damn!" Her face was burning as she tried to fish the broken glass out of the soapy water. She could feel his gaze on her.

"Noah?" He said his name with quiet speculation.

"I could call him something else while you're here," Susannah offered.

But Noah shook his head. He hunkered down carefully and scratched the cat behind the ears, then looked up at Susannah. "Did you name him after me?"

"Uh-huh," said Susannah.

At the same time, Tess blurted, "Not really."

"Because he was a stray," Susannah went on earnestly, while Tess wished the floor would open and swallow her up. "Mom said it was a good name because we couldn't count on him sticking around."

Noah's eyes turned to Tess. His smile faded.

Serves you right, Tess thought grimly as she dared to meet his gaze. In the stillness, Noah-the-cat purred madly and rubbed his head against Noah-the-cowboy's leg.

"But he's still here," Susannah said after a moment into the tense silence. "And it's been two years." Tess could almost see wheels turning in her daughter's head.

"Because he knows a pair of suckers when he sees them," Tess said flatly. "Right, cat?"

"Because he loves us," Susannah contradicted her stoutly. Her gaze went from the cat to her father.

Tess smothered a groan. She dropped the broken glass into the trash. "I think it's time we went looking for that tree."

Tess had a five-year-old Ford Bronco, a good snow car. Susannah climbed into the back. After stowing his crutches, Noah settled in front. Tess drove. No one spoke until they were inside the grocery store. Then Noah watched and listened as Tess and Susannah discussed the week's grocery purchases.

"What kind of cereal do you like?" Susannah asked him at one point "I like this—" she held up a colorful sugared variety "—but Mom says it isn't good for me. It has the same vitamins as the other stuff. I told her that, but she won't believe me. Do you believe me?"

"I didn't say it didn't have the same vitamins," Tess said firmly. "I said it isn't as good for your teeth. Put it back, Suse."

Susannah looked at Noah beseechingly. Noah looked at her mother. It wasn't hard to read Tess's expression: *buck me on this and you're outa here.*

"It's a little too sweet," he told Susannah.

Her face fell. "But it's Christmas," she argued in a last-ditch effort.

"We don't get *everything* we want at Christmas," Tess said. "And you, young lady, have gotten quite enough." She turned then and pushed the cart briskly down the aisle.

Susannah hung back to walk with Noah. "She's not always this crabby," the little girl confided. "Usually she's pretty nice."

"Yeah," Noah said wistfully. "I know."

If he wasn't much use in the grocery store, he was even less so when it came to putting the bags in the car. By the time he navigated through the ever-deepening snow and stowed his crutches, then turned to help, Tess had the bags already loaded in the back and was waiting for him to get in.

Tess handled the Bronco easily through the accumulating snow. But as they slid when they came to a stoplight, Noah flinched, the memories of the trailer all too vivid.

Tess glanced over. "Sorry about that. Are you okay?" And for the first time he heard the soft note of concern in her voice that he remembered from eight years before.

"Yeah. Sure." He shrugged and tried to pretend his heart wasn't slamming against the wall of his chest. "Just a little skittish, I guess."

"Taggart said you saw it coming?"

"Uh-huh. Scared me sh—a lot."

Susannah leaned forward. "What scared you?"

"I was in a car accident. That's why I've got crutches."

Her eyes got big. "I thought you got that from riding a bronc. What happened?"

He told her briefly, glossing over the gorier bits as her eyes got wider and wider and her worried expression grew. Her lower lip trembled and she ran her tongue over it. "You're . . . you're not gonna die or anything, are you?"

"I'm not gonna die."

She seemed to breathe a little easier, but she still regarded him with obvious concern. Her hand crept up between the seats to clutch his. He turned farther around in the seat and gave her a smile.

"I'm fine, Susannah," he said again as Tess pulled the Bronco alongside a lot filled with Christmas trees. "I've never been better." And he was surprised to find that it was true. He'd stopped feeling sorry for himself somewhere around the time he'd discovered he was a father. He hadn't had a second to bemoan his fate since. Now he didn't want to.

He climbed out and leaned on his crutches, watching as Susannah, reassured, forgot all about him and ran into the forest of Christmas trees, scanning them for the perfect one.

Tess came around the car slowly, as if she expected him to jump down her throat the moment he got her alone.

Probably she did. And a part of him wanted to. Every time he stopped to think about Susannah, he wanted to rage at Tess. How could she have kept it from him? he demanded silently. Another part of him knew the fault was entirely his.

In any case, they could hardly discuss it now.

Noah drew a deep breath and let it out slowly. "She's beautiful," he said. They stood side by side, not touching.

Noah could see Tess's hands jammed into the pockets of her down jacket. Snowflakes dusted her hair and turned to silver drops of moisture on her long dark lashes. Under the lights of the Christmas-tree lot, he could see the color in her cheeks, blurring her freckles into a rosy gold. Susannah wasn't the only one who was beautiful, he thought, tightening his own hands into fists as he resisted the urge to touch her.

Tess nodded, a faint smile lighting her face. "She is."

Susannah popped out from between two trees, waving wildly. "Come look at this one!"

"If it's hard for you to walk, you can wait in the car," Tess said.

One of Noah's crutches skidded on an icy patch. He didn't care. He wouldn't have missed this for the world.

"You're right, it's lovely," Tess was saying to Susannah when he finally reached them. It was an eight-foot tree, thick and well-formed and bushy. A perfect tree, as far as Noah could see. "But it's too big."

Susannah's face fell. "Why? Why is it too big?"

"We'd have to cut off three feet to get it on the table—"

"We don't need a table. Why can't we get a floor tree? We always have one of those little-bitty trees." Susannah looked up at her mother pleadingly.

Tess brushed a hand over Susannah's dark hair. "Little-bitty trees need families to love them, too."

Susannah's lower lip jutted out. "I know. But we've loved *lots* of little trees. Please, Mommy! Just this year?" She looked at her mother beseechingly, then turned to Noah. "Don't *you* think it's great?"

"It's great," Noah agreed.

Tess shot him a dirty look. "Suse, it's beautiful. I know that. But we can't af—" She stopped, biting off what she'd intended to say. "We just can't," she said flatly.

Susannah's small shoulders slumped. She kicked at the snow with the toe of one of her white, fur-topped boots. "I know," she mumbled.

Noah didn't have much trouble hearing what neither of them was saying: it was a great tree, but it was too expensive. But he knew Tess was damned if she was going to say that in front of him.

He could afford the tree—hell, this year he could afford a dozen tress—but he knew better than to offer. He glanced around for an alternative.

"*I'm* buying the tree," Tess said to him through gritted teeth in a tone pitched too softly for Susannah to hear.

"Fine, you buy the tree," Noah agreed. "What about that one?" He nodded toward an even taller tree that was full and bushy on one side, but had a rather obvious bare spot on the other. "It's not perfect," he said before Susannah could point that out, "but it's big. And if we put that side in the corner . . ." He deliberately didn't look at Tess.

He heard her draw a breath as if she might argue, but then she let it out again and didn't say a word.

Susannah, too, started to say something, then stopped. She approached the tree cautiously, as if getting too close might be a mistake. She wasn't smiling, but she did seem intrigued. Noah left Tess standing where she was and hobbled over to stand by Susannah. She was looking at the tree thoughtfully.

"You think they might sell it for less 'cause it's got this hole?" She slanted a glance up at him.

"I think they might. Want me to ask?"

She glanced over at her mother. Some imperceptible communication passed between mother and daughter. Then Susannah looked back up at him. "Yes."

Noah went to find the owner. He frankly didn't care if the guy wanted more—it was going to look like less, Tess was going to save face and Susannah was going to have her tree.

The owner, however, took one look at the tree and agreed. "Be nice to give this one a good home," he said, as he carried it to the car for them. He even provided a couple of stout pieces of twine, which Noah used to lash it on top of the Bronco while Tess took out her billfold and paid.

Susannah bounced excitedly all the way home. "We got a floor tree! We got a floor tree!" she chanted over and over.

Tess didn't say a word. When they got to the house, Susannah helped her carry the tree into the house. Noah limped along behind on his crutches and hoped he'd done the right thing.

It didn't take long to find out. Once the tree was up and turned properly, its top nearly brushing the ceiling, Susannah's eyes sparkled and her smile seemed to cover her whole face. It didn't matter that there was a hole in the back. It didn't matter that the trunk was the slightest bit crooked.

"Come look, Mommy!" she yelled.

And when Tess came to the doorway from the kitchen, Susannah said, "Look! It's the biggest, most beautiful tree in the world!"

Tess looked at the tree, then at her daughter and, finally, at Noah. Did her gaze soften at all or was he dreaming it? "So it is," she said. "So it is."

Susannah didn't want to go to sleep. She wanted to decorate the tree.

"Tomorrow," Tess said firmly when the little girl was in pajamas and slippers and still pleading. She'd had enough for one day.

"All of us?" Susannah asked, her gaze flickering to Noah, who has been sitting at the kitchen table nursing a cup of coffee Tess had given him to drink while she supervised Susannah's getting ready for bed. She didn't need him hovering there, too.

"What?" Tess said, distracted even now by his presence.

"Can we all decorate it?" Susannah repeated. "You an' me an'..." Her voice faded as she looked hopefully at her father. It was as if she thought that once she shut her eyes, Noah would disappear.

Tess drew a deep breath and squelched the wish that he would. "Yes," she said, "all of us."

Susannah nodded. "That's all right then." She looked at Noah. "Will you tuck me in?"

Her request made him sit up straight, and Tess saw his fingers tighten on the coffee mug. "Tuck you in?" His gaze met Tess's. He looked apprehensive.

Good, she thought. She hoped he'd say no. He didn't.

"Sure," he said, and carefully pushed himself to his feet. "I'd like that."

Susannah beamed as he led the way into the hall and up the steps. She stopped at the doorway. "You, too, Mommy."

Tess hesitated. She didn't want to. Oh Lord, she didn't want to. It would be another dream laid low by reality—she and Noah together at their daughter's bedside.

But Susannah was waiting, and it was a ritual. Tess swallowed, then nodded her head.

Susannah beat them both to her room. She'd already scrambled into her bed, her small mouth curving into a satisfied smile as she looked from one parent to the other. Then she held out a hand to Noah. Awkwardly, he took it. She held out the other to her mother. Tess wrapped the small fingers in her own.

Susannah gave a satisfied sigh. "Good."

"Good night," Tess said firmly, and bent to drop a kiss on her daughter's mouth. Small, strong arms went around her neck, tugging her down so Susannah could give her a smacking kiss. "Night, Mommy." The look of pure, impish joy in her daughter's eyes made Tess's throat tighten.

"Sweet dreams, sweetheart," she whispered. *Don't let him hurt her,* she prayed. *Please don't let him hurt her.* Then she loosed her hand and stepped back as her daughter turned to Noah.

He looked as serious as she could ever remember seeing him. Tess wondered if he had any inkling what having a daughter meant. Did he even have a clue about the joys and the pains, the comforts and the responsibilities of parenting such a marvelous child?

Of course he didn't. He couldn't. He'd only known of her existence for a few short hours. He knew nothing about children at all.

But now that he knew about Susannah, what would he do?

An evening, a meal, a hunt for a Christmas tree were all well and good, but they meant nothing in the long run.

Of course, tomorrow he would still be here. He'd promised. So had she.

But after?

It didn't take a mind reader to know that Susannah wanted him forever.

Noah? Forever?

How likely was that?

Still, Tess's heart squeezed inside her chest when she saw him smile a little crookedly as he looked down at the little girl. "Night, Susannah," he said softly.

She took his hand again and tugged on it, pulling him toward her. He went down on one knee, oddly shy and rather clumsy, Tess thought, though it could have been because of his injuries.

He bent his head. And then he touched his lips to hers.

It was a sweet kiss. Gentle. Tender. A father's kiss.

Tess's eyes brimmed.

It was over in scant seconds. She saw a shudder ripple down Noah's spine as he drew back and started to stand. But Susannah's hand came up and held him still. Her fingers brushed against the day's growth of whiskers on his cheek, lingering for a moment. Then she smiled again. The look she gave Noah was one of such complete trust and childlike faith that Tess's heart wrenched in her chest.

"I knew you'd come," Susannah said.

Four

Neither of them spoke as they left Susannah's room. Neither said a word all the way back down the hall, down the stairs and into the living room. But both of them knew what was next.

It was the moment of reckoning—the first time in eight years that all the cards were on the table.

Noah thanked God at least he knew what game they were playing for a change, even though he still didn't have a clue where to begin. But if, as Susannah thought, God was involved in this, He'd provide the clues.

But He hadn't by the time they reached the living room, and there was nowhere else to go. God might be there, but He sure wasn't taking sides or directing the scene.

So it was up to him and Tess.

She stood in the doorway, looking at him with a gaze that combined apprehension and belligerence. With her feet slightly apart and her fingers curled at her sides, she reminded him of a mother bear ready to defend her cub.

And damn it all, a part of Noah wanted to attack her! He wanted to shake her and demand to know what she'd thought she was doing, keeping Susannah a secret from him all these years!

The saner, more rational part of him knew exactly what she'd been doing—showing good sense.

As much as it pained him to admit it even to himself—*especially* to himself—he knew exactly what had motivated her; and he knew she'd been right. He'd been no more ready to be a father eight years ago than he'd been to be a husband. He'd have made a mess of all three of their lives if she'd given him the chance.

He knew it. But knowing and accepting the truth of it didn't make it any easier to bear. He muttered an expletive under his breath.

"Well, too damn bad," Tess snapped, misunderstanding completely the source of his disgust. She slapped her hands on her hips. "I realize this isn't what you had in mind when you showed up on my doorstep. I suppose all you really wanted was a roll in the hay. Well, sorry, fella, you got a daughter instead."

"I don't—"

"A daughter doesn't exactly fit into your life-style, does she?" Tess went on without giving him a chance to protest. "Well, too bad, buddy boy. That's life!" Her eyes flashed. She glared. "And you have only yourself to blame. If you hadn't come nosing around, you wouldn't even know. God knows, I tried to keep it from you. I tried to protect you! And her," she added heavily after a moment.

All her flash and fire vanished as suddenly as it had come, leaving her burned out and weary looking. Tess sighed and rubbed a hand over her eyes, looking lonelier and sadder than Noah had ever seen her.

An odd, tight feeling grabbed at his chest. "You shouldn't have," he said gruffly. "Tried to protect me, I mean."

"You think it would have been better to have told you?" Her tone clearly told him she did not.

He shoved a hand through his hair, ruffling it. "I might've been worth somethin' to you. I could've helped you financially, at least."

"I didn't want your help. Not after—" She stopped.

"After what?"

"After your phone call. Surely you remember it? The one where you said, 'Oh, by the way, I'm never coming back'?"

"You knew? You knew then?"

"It had been two months!"

"I know! But I— Hell. You must've hated me."

"It would've been easier."

He looked at her closely. "Why didn't you just tell me? Blurt it out? I deserved it."

"Maybe. But we didn't."

He had the grace to flush. He stared at his boot tops, feeling lower than a cow pie, more incompetent than a newborn colt. "I could've helped," he said finally, desperately.

"I managed without your help." Her gaze flickered around their comfortable, albeit somewhat worn, surroundings, and she lifted her chin. "Susannah didn't do without anything important."

"Just her father."

"Damn you! You didn't want me! Why would you have wanted her?"

"I didn't mean it like that. I didn't, really. I'm sorry, Tess. It just...just came out." He moved toward her. When she backed up, he stopped where he was. "You're right. I can

see she's fine. You've done fine. It's just that—'' he sighed
''—hell, I don't know. I never expected this.''

In the Teflon days of his youth, his actions had never had
consequences. At least, he hadn't thought so. Clearly he'd
been wrong. Noah turned his back on her and limped to the
far end of the room, needing air, space; feeling as if the walls
were coming in on him. He muttered under his breath again,
turned too quickly, tripped and almost fell.

"You ought to sit down," Tess said automatically.

"Before I fall down, you mean?" he said wryly.

She didn't smile, but her expression softened slightly.
"Yes."

She was right. His leg was killing him. Leaning on the
crutches for any length of time made his elbow and shoulder ache. Doing without them was dangerous as hell. So he
sat. He slumped back against the couch and closed his eyes.
He tried to think of what to say, what to do. All his mind
could manage was replaying for the hundredth time the
moment of revelation he'd had that afternoon. He could still
see Susannah as she'd looked making the snowman when
he'd arrived. Could still see the dark-haired, anonymous
child he'd thought might be Tess's niece.

He shook his head, then opened his eyes. "That's why
you were avoiding me all the time at the hospital."

She hesitated, then nodded.

"Would you ever have told me?"

"Maybe. Someday." She walked to the fireplace and
picked up the glass snow globe on the mantel, staring into
its swirling whiteness. "Susannah could have told you herself when she was grown—if she wanted to."

"Would you have told me in Cheyenne . . . if you hadn't
seen me in the midway?"

Her knuckles whitened on the globe. "She wanted to go.
I didn't."

"She told me that, too. Would you?" he persisted

"I . . . I don't know."

"You thought Maggie was my wife?"

Tess didn't reply. She was looking at the globe again, but he saw her nod almost imperceptibly.

"Was that the other reason you didn't say anything this past week?"

Another faint nod.

"You thought I'd be coming on to you if I was married?"

"I didn't think! I didn't want to think!" She almost slammed the globe back on the mantel and spun to face him. "I didn't let myself think," she amended flatly. "I tried my best not to think about you at all."

The silence that followed was broken only by the snap and crack of the fire. Noah-the-cat came into the living room and wound through Tess's ankles, purring. Noah could hear him clear across the room.

"Tess," he said quietly, "you gotta know I didn't mean to hurt you. It isn't that I didn't want to come back. I did. But it wouldn't have worked. You know that. I couldn't stay. I just—just . . . would've left you again. And again."

"I know. As you reminded me, you never made any promises." She shrugged. "But I was young and foolish, and I simply couldn't keep from hoping."

The look on her face sent a knife right through him.

"I was trying—this time—not to be old and foolish," she said quietly. "For Susannah's sake mostly, but also for my own."

"I won't hurt you again," he promised.

For a long moment Tess just looked at him. "No. You won't," she said. "Because I won't let you. But I can't prevent you from hurting Susannah."

"You can't think I'd do anything to hurt her!"

"I don't see how you can help it. I mean, here you are—" Tess's mouth twisted "—the answer to her prayer. And I know Suse well enough to know that it won't stop there. She'll be praying for you to stay. I know she will. And then what'll happen?"

I'll stay, Noah wanted to say. But he knew better than to promise such a thing. Hell, he hadn't stayed anywhere for longer than two weeks since he'd turned eighteen. He looked at Tess helplessly. "I don't know."

Tess sighed. She sagged into the lumpy armchair and hauled the cat up onto her lap. "I don't know, either," she said. She didn't look at him. Instead, she sat watching her fingers scratch behind the cat's ears.

A log shifted in the grate. The flames flickered, then ebbed to a low orange glow. Noah stared at it, then at Tess. He shoved his hands into the pockets of his jeans. Then he tipped his head back and shut his eyes.

If he'd given any thought to how he and Tess might spend their first evening together in over eight years, he'd thought in terms of a little apologizing, followed by a little cuddling, a little kissing and then—with the best of cowboy luck—a little making up for lost time.

He'd never, ever, imagined them sitting at opposite ends of the living room, each absorbed in thought, neither sure exactly how to deal with the other—or with the daughter who inextricably bound them.

"Is he still here?"

"Shh. Yes, of course he's still here."

"In your bedroom?"

"Shh. Yes, in my bedroom. It's where I put Uncle Philip and Aunt Nancy."

"Did you *sleep* with him?"

"Shh! No, I did not!"

"Oh."

Tess didn't have to shush her this time. All the eagerness, all the enthusiasm, all the awe and hope that Noah had heard in Susannah's voice died in that one small word.

Noah rolled carefully onto his side so he could see whatever was visible through the thin crack of light that shone from the hallway outside the room Tess had given him for the night. He had protested that he could sleep on the couch. He—unlike Susannah—had had no illusions that they might share Tess's bed.

"No," she'd said quite firmly. "I want you in there. It will keep you out of the way."

Put like that, how could he refuse?

Now he saw an eye pressed against the crack in the door. He winked at it.

"He's awake!" Susannah started to open the door.

It banged soundly shut again. "Enough," he heard Tess say fiercely. "You can not just barge in on company."

"He's not company. He's my father!" Susannah argued.

"He's still company," Tess said.

And damned well going to stay that way, Noah heard unspoken but all too loud and clear in Tess's tone.

Then her voice softened slightly. "He doesn't—I mean, no one likes being bothered when they just wake up, Suse."

"But—"

"You can see him when he gets up. Now leave him in peace and come eat your breakfast."

"But—" But Susannah, still managing feeble protests, was apparently hauled away.

Noah rolled onto his back, shoved himself up against the headboard of Tess's bed and smiled. Why? Because he knew what she'd intended to say before she'd caught herself. *He doesn't like getting up in the morning. He's a grouch. A regular pain in the neck.*

And she would know. Oh yes, she would know. She'd teased him about it often enough. And she remembered, too. Even if she didn't want to.

Noah's smile widened.

Tess's bed was a full-size double, but just barely. It was not the sort of bed that gave the notion she spent much time in it—or did anything other than sleep when she was there. He wasn't surprised.

He *was* pleased, and that did surprise him.

He'd never given much thought to what the women he'd known had done when they weren't doing it with him. But he found he was gratified to discover that Tess, at least in her own bed, very likely hadn't been doing much of anything.

Her room was, in fact, only slightly less austere than a nun's room would be. A utilitarian, old oak dresser, chosen, he was sure, because of its functionality and not its antique value, stood against the far wall. There was a walk-in closet barely big enough for a child of Susannah's size to turn around in. And beside the bed, she had placed a small table on which there was a digital alarm clock, a rather battered paperback Tony Hillerman mystery and a framed snapshot of a somewhat-younger Susannah riding high on a playground swing, dark hair flying in the breeze. No pictures of him.

Curiously and unjustifiably, he felt nettled. Had he wanted her pining after him for eight years, for God's sake? He hadn't pined after her. Not after the first few months, anyway. Other than a momentary twinge every time he came close to Laramie, months would go by without him thinking of her.

He knew she'd remembered him every single day. And, he thought grimly, she hadn't needed a picture to do it.

Had she resented Susannah's entrance into her life? Certainly she hadn't wanted a baby. Not then, anyway. And certainly not under those circumstances. She'd been almost finished with her nurse's training when they'd met. She'd had grand notions of going on for an academic degree, perhaps even a master's, and then teaching.

Obviously she wasn't teaching. He wondered if she'd been able to realize any of her plans with a child to support.

Guilt washed over him once more. Damn it, she should have asked him for help!

Yeah, right, his more rational side responded. You were making such big bucks in those days. Eight years ago he'd barely been breaking even on the circuit. Gasoline and other traveling expenses, not to mention the fees he paid to compete, had eaten virtually all of his meager earnings.

Only in the last five years had he begun to see a bit of daylight in the profit department. If Tess had asked him for money in the early days, well, he'd have had to give up rodeoing, that was certain.

And then there would have been two of them who'd lost the chance to pursue their dreams.

The enormity of how much he owed her was borne in on him again.

Then, hearing Susannah's childish giggle downstairs, he realized that though he'd had his freedom, he'd lost something, too. And as much as he'd have liked to, he couldn't blame Tess for denying him. Not when he'd denied her first.

He sighed and hauled himself out of bed, pulling on a clean pair of jeans, then hobbling toward the bathroom to shave. When he finished, he stood staring at his reflection in the mirror, looking for signs of fatherhood, maturity, responsibility. It wasn't promising.

Susannah was sitting at the table, eating a bowl of oatmeal, and Tess was taking pieces of toast out of the toaster.

Both of them looked up when he came into the kitchen. Susannah grinned. Tess turned away.

"I didn't think you were ever getting up. Did you see all the snow?" Susannah asked him, all eager enthusiasm. She shoved her chair back and went to the window, pointing. "Look."

Obediently Noah looked. There was at least a foot of snow on the ground and it was still coming down.

Susannah looked at him hopefully. "Want to help me make another snowman?"

"Noah's hurt," Tess said without turning around.

"I reckon I could manage a little helping," Noah said. "After breakfast?"

"Libby's coming over to play after breakfast," Tess said. She was talking to the toast. "She and Jeff, so their mom can go do some Christmas shopping."

"They can help, too." Susannah shrugged her shoulders. "Libby's eight. She lives next door," she told Noah. "You don't care, do you? Her dad lets me do things with them sometimes," she added.

"I don't mind," he said. "That's fine. I'd like to meet her." *And her father,* he thought, feeling a vague resentment toward any man who habitually did things with his daughter.

Tess gave him an irritated look. He met it levelly. He knew she thought he was just saying what Susannah wanted to hear. Tess herself didn't want to hear that he actually was eager to meet Susannah's friend.

But he was. He was curious about a lot of things. Susannah's friend was simply one of them.

Tess set a plate of toast in front of him on the table. "Sit down and eat."

She looked tired, as if she hadn't slept any better than he had. He wanted to reach out and touch her, soothe her the way he knew he could. But he knew better.

Instead he nodded and sat down at the table across from Susannah. "Thanks."

"Then later we can decorate the tree," Susannah went on. If she was aware of the undercurrents in the room, she gave no sign. "Mommy makes cookies to hang on it," she told Noah. "Snowmen and Santas and angels and stuff. An' I've got the ornaments my aunt Nancy sends me. You wanta see 'em?" She was halfway out of her chair when Tess pressed a hand on her shoulder.

"Finish your breakfast. You can show him later."

"But—"

"You can show me later," Noah assured her around a mouthful of toast.

Susannah settled back in her chair. "'Cause you're gonna be here," she said with satisfaction.

They had barely finished breakfast when there was a knock on the door. Tess opened it, and a girl about Susannah's age came in.

"This is Libby," Susannah said. "This," she told Libby, "is Noah."

Libby blinked. "Noah? *The* Noah?" Obviously he'd been the topic of discussion in the past. Noah shifted uncomfortably under the girl's scrutiny. "Your... father?"

Susannah nodded, smiling all over her face. "My father."

Libby's eyes got saucer size as she stared at Noah. He smiled at her. Her eyes got even wider. She looked from him to Susannah. "You did it," she said to her friend, her voice an awed, hushed whisper. "How?"

Susannah shrugged. "Dunno for sure. I was makin' a snowman an' a taxi brought him."

"Wow."

Tess clattered the cereal pot in the sink. "Oh, for heaven's sake. He was just getting out of the hospital and he needed someplace to go. Susannah, hurry up and finish your breakfast. Libby, where's Jeff?"

"He went to Mark's. Aren'tcha glad? I am. Mom says she'll be back by noon if you can stand me that long."

"We'll see," Tess said dryly.

Susannah slurped the milk out of her cereal bowl and carried it to the sink. "He's gonna help us with the snowman," she told Libby, tipping her head in Noah's direction. "But we gotta be careful of him 'cause, like Mom said, he just got out of the hospital and he's still sorta hurt."

Libby glanced shyly at Noah once more, then nodded.

Susannah hovered by his arm. "So will you be ready soon?" she asked.

"Don't pester," Tess said, trying to fish a piece of toast out of the toaster.

Susannah sighed, but then grabbed Libby's arm and hauled her toward the bedroom. "Come on," she said. As they disappeared, Noah heard her telling Libby, "Last night he helped us get a tree. An'," she added confidentially, "he slept in my mom's bed."

"Damn it!" Tess dropped the burned toast and popped blistered fingers into her mouth. She glared at Noah. "It's not funny!"

"Am I laughing?"

"You're smiling," she accused him.

"Sorry." He ran a hand down his face in an unsuccessful attempt to wipe off the grin. "C'mon, Tess," he said, pushing himself to his feet and moving back from the table. "You gotta admit there is a humorous element to it."

She turned away. "Maybe to you."

He hobbled over to her, cornering her between the refrigerator and the cabinets. "Hey," he said softly, touching her arm, turning her so that, even though she momentarily resisted, she finally faced him. "It's gonna be okay. She's not implying anything. At least I don't think she is—or not what you're thinking, anyway. Don't take everything so seriously. She's just a kid."

"She's *my* kid. And yours," she added grimly. "And she wants things she can't have!"

"So, she'll learn. We all do."

Tess tried to shrug away from him. "Easy for you to say. You're not going to be here to pick up the pieces."

"You think I'm going to stay around till Christmas, then just disappear?"

"You did before."

Her words stung, but he kept his face impassive. "I called."

"And said you weren't coming back."

"You could've told me."

"Why should I have when you clearly didn't want to be bothered?"

He pressed his lips together, but didn't answer. There was no answer, and they both knew it.

"Anyway, I didn't want you." She did push past him then, picking up the milk carton and opening the refrigerator door. "I still don't."

Her words hurt. And it didn't even help much to know she was lying. He wondered if she knew it. He wanted her to. "Don't you?" He challenged her softly, a brow arching as he looked at her. He remembered the kiss in the hospital and knew from the flame of color in her cheeks that she was remembering it, too.

Tess shut her eyes. He saw her fists clench at her sides. She drew a careful breath. "Don't do this," she said. The pain on her face was clear. "Please. Don't."

It was another one of her dreams—to stand in the window and watch Susannah and her father playing together in the snow.

Noah wasn't much good at rolling snowballs into body parts. Tess could tell that his ribs didn't like all that bending over. And his crutches didn't provide the best support on ice, either. Words of warning rose in her throat several times, but she wouldn't go to the door and say something. It was none of her business, after all.

Certainly Noah didn't move as easily as the girls did, but even when he wasn't helping, he stood watching Susannah and her friend as they labored, their cheeks turning bright red as they scampered around the small yard. He seemed enchanted, his gaze rapt as he leaned on his crutches, smiling, the ever-present wind tousling his dark hair and putting color back in his lean cheeks. He was still the handsomest man she'd ever seen.

Tess turned away. She was going to make cookie dough this morning, then chill it enough so they could cut out cookies this afternoon. She had no time to stand at the window gawking.

Somehow, she couldn't help herself. She was mixing sugar and eggs, flour and baking soda, butter and orange rind and mace. But she was moving back and forth from the table to the window as she did so. Checking on Susannah, she told herself. Keeping an eye on Libby, like a good baby-sitter should. What else?

She noticed that the girls were a little shy at first when they discovered that Noah couldn't do much in the way of helping. They became rather self-conscious, slanting him wary glances, but not speaking to him.

But then, when the snowman was finished, they started throwing snowballs at it and at each other. It was only a matter of time until Libby's poor aim made Noah part of the action.

One moment he was standing there watching, and the next he got a fat, sloppy snowball square in the chest.

"Oh!" Susannah shrieked, clapping her hand over her mouth.

Both girls stopped dead and looked at him nervously.

They looked so terrified that Tess saw Noah grin. She remembered that grin—the hint that devilish mischief was about to befall someone. Slowly he scraped the snow off his jacket and began shaping it into a smaller, but still good-size, ball.

Neither girl moved. Then, taking careful aim, the grin spreading across his face as he did so, he threw the snowball at Susannah.

It hit her lightly on the top of her fuzzy pompom cap, and a cascade of wet snow dripped onto her lashes.

She giggled. She shook her head and wiped the snow off her face. Then, giving him a look filled with purely feminine wiles, she scooped up a ball of snow and flung it back.

The fight was on.

The odds were against him, and Tess was sure he knew it. Two bright-eyed, healthy, rambunctious grade-school girls were more than a match for a gimpy-legged, cracked-ribbed man, even one in his prime. But still, he gave, if not as good as he got, as good as he could. And Tess, because she was alone, was free to enjoy the spectacle. She rooted for the girls, giggling when one of them hit him on the back of the head with a large, fluffy ball that sent a cascade of snow down inside his jacket.

Tess laughed as she saw him squirm, then bend to scoop some more snow. He might have even held his own if his crutch hadn't slipped. But when he tried to catch himself, he twisted, skidded and landed flat on his back.

"Mom!"

"Ms. Montgom'ry!"

"Ma! Come quick!"

But they didn't have to say a word. Tess was already flying out the door.

She crouched beside him and lay a hand on his chest. "Don't move!"

Noah was struggling to get up. "I'm okay!"

"You're not. You could have broken—"

"I didn't break anything. I ride broncs for a living. I fall every day of my life." He looked equal parts irritated and mortified.

Tess didn't care. "Not on the ice. Not like this." She started patting him down, running her hands over him.

All of a sudden Noah sank back onto the ground and groaned.

"What is it?" she demanded.

Susannah and Libby looked immediately alarmed. "Did we kill him?"

"Of course not," Tess said sharply. But she was moving quickly as she unzipped his jacket and started unbuttoning his shirt. He could have reinjured his ribs. One of them could have repunctured his lung. Her hands pressed against his bare chest. "Where does it hurt?"

"Lower."

Her fingers moved down to the base of his rib cage. "There?"

"No."

They skimmed around toward his sides. "Now?"

He shook his head. "Hm-mm. Lower." She could feel his breath stirring her hair as she bent over him.

"Where?" Her hands stilled momentarily. She raised her head to look at him.

He met her gaze, then dropped his in the general direction of the fly of his jeans.

Tess's face flamed. She sat back abruptly on her heels, put both hands against his chest and shoved him flat.

"Hey!"

"Mom!"

But Tess was already on her feet and heading back to the house as fast as she had come.

"Tess! I was kidding! Tess!"

She paused only long enough to scoop up a huge handful of snow. Her aim was better than the girls'. She got him square in the face!

The sound of the slamming door echoed all over Laramie. Noah reached up and wiped the remains of the snowball off his face. Susannah and Libby were staring at him, their jaws sagging, their eyes like dinner plates.

"She was kidding, too," Noah said to them as he struggled to get to his feet. His ribs hurt like hell. He knew Tess would tell him he deserved it. "Give me a hand, Suse."

The little girl reached out and, together, they got him to his feet. Both she and Libby brushed the snow off him, doing more smacking than dusting. Probably Tess would figure he deserved that, too.

"I don't think she was kidding. I think she was mad at you," Susannah told him solemnly when they'd finished. She looked worried. "But I don't know why." She looked at him for an explanation.

He couldn't begin to give her one.

"Do you think she'll make you leave?" she asked a bit fearfully.

And Noah realized she was worried that he might. She couldn't possibly understand what was happening between him and Tess. She only knew that she—and her wish for her father—might end up a victim of their disharmony.

"No," Noah said firmly. "She won't make me leave."

"How do you know?"

"Because she's your mother and she wants the best for you." He was certain of that.

"But—"

"And I'll ask her not to."

Susannah swallowed. "Truly?"

Noah nodded.

"When?"

He contemplated the front door. In his ears he could still hear it slamming. In his mind's eye he could still see Tess's worried face as she bent over him, could still feel her hands on him, arousing him when he had no business being aroused, making him say things he had no right to say.

He knew he ought to give her time to cool off. But then he looked down into a pair of bright blue eyes, worried, waiting, hoping.

"Now," he said.

Five

___

"Tess?"

There was no answer. Noah left his boots in the entry hall, hung his jacket on one of the hooks just inside the front door and headed toward the kitchen. There was a bowl of dry ingredients for cookie dough on the table, a carton of eggs next to the bowl, a half-grated orange rind sitting on a plate. No Tess.

"Tess?" he called a little louder.

She didn't reply.

She wasn't in the living room or the tiny dining area. He hesitated, then started up the narrow stairs. She wasn't in her bedroom or the bathroom. A small sound came from Susannah's room, beyond the half-closed door. Noah went to the door and pushed it open. Tess stood with her back to him, her shoulders still hunched as she stared out the window toward the backyard.

"I'm sorry."

Her shoulders lifted in a stiff shrug. "Yeah, sure." Her voice wobbled, then cracked. She sounded as if she'd been crying. Something twisted deep in his gut. He came up behind her and would have touched her, except he was sure she would have flinched away.

"Come on, Tess. It was a joke. I—"

She whirled around to face him. He could see the track of a tear down her cheek. "It's always a joke with you, isn't it, Noah? Well, damn it, maybe I should laugh, but *I can't!*" She tried to spin away again, to duck past him and run out of the room. He grabbed her before she could.

"Aw, hell," he whispered, dragging her stiff, resisting body against his, holding her prisoner there. "I can't help it, Tess. I don't want to joke. I have to."

She continued to struggle for a moment, then sagged onto his chest. "What's that mean?" she muttered into the fabric of his shirt. Her question was equal parts caution and doubt.

He shrugged awkwardly. "It just...seems easier. I don't do too well at the deep stuff. Sayin' what I feel." Even this was hard. The words felt like lead he was hauling up all the way from his toes.

She backed up a fraction of an inch and lifted her gaze to connect with his. "You're saying it's a defense mechanism?"

He didn't know the term, but it sounded about right. "I guess." God, he was drowning in those green eyes of hers. He wanted her desperately; she had to know that. But he wanted her to know it was more than just desiring her body—because, damn it, it was.

"So try," she prompted. "Tell me...what are you feeling now?"

He scratched his ear, reluctant, but knowing she was waiting and that he owed her that much at least. "Incompetent." A corner of his mouth tilted wryly. "Out of my depth. Horny?" he added after a moment, then grimaced. "See? It's always easier to talk about sex."

Tess shook her head. "For you. Not for me."

"No. Probably not," he allowed. "But then, you've always been a better person than me."

"Don't say that."

"It's true. Anyhow, I'm sorry for teasing you out there. You were worried and I appreciate it. I know you'd...rather not be."

She looked at him almost shamefacedly for a moment, then glanced away.

"I want you to care," he said earnestly. And because he owed her complete honesty, he added, "But I'm afraid of it, too."

She looked at him then. "Because it imposes obligations." She didn't make it a question.

He traced a circle with his tongue on the inside of his cheek and looked down at the toes of his boots. "Yeah."

"I'm not asking you for anything."

"I know."

She sighed. "But Susannah is."

"Not really. Well—" he hesitated "—she is sort of afraid you're gonna send me away."

"As if I dared."

"I told her you wouldn't."

Tess gave him an arch look. "How's that for confidence."

"Not because of me," he said quickly. He loosed his hands from behind her and laid them on her shoulders. "Because you love her."

"More than anything in the world," Tess said fiercely. She stepped away from him and went to stare out the window.

"I know that," he said quietly. "She's a lucky kid."

Tess turned and met his gaze. They stared at each other.

Noah remembered the first time he'd looked deep into Tess Montgomery's eyes eight years before, he'd been young and stupid and out of his depth in the face of her passion and intelligence and hope and, yes, love. He'd taken them all as his due, barely even thinking about them—about her.

Now as he stepped forward, lifted a hand and, with a knuckle, grazed Tess's cheek lightly, he began to understand how much he had lost. Not just Susannah.

Her mother. Tess.

He swallowed hard against the lump in his throat, then ran his tongue lightly over his lips. "Thanks," he said softly.

She gave him a quizzical look.

"For still caring."

Her fingers knotted together. "I can't help it," she said.

It was only since Tanner had married Maggie that Noah had really begun to celebrate Christmas again. Until he'd started spending the holiday with them, the memories he'd stored up from his childhood—memories of cookie baking and house decorating and tree trimming and church going—had seemed locked away, frozen in the ice of a past too far removed to bring back.

To be honest, he hadn't *wanted* to bring them back. They hurt too much.

But the warmth and love he'd found in Tanner and Maggie's first Christmas together had begun melting the ice around those memories and washing away sharp edges of remembered pain. Each subsequent Christmas had freed them up a bit more.

But nothing had prepared Noah for the veritable flood of feelings and memories this Christmas brought him.

He went back outside, ostensibly to supervise the girls, but mostly to put some distance between himself and Tess. They weren't in the backyard where he'd left them, but he could hear girlish voices around front, so he limped that way.

"Look!" Susannah called to him. As he watched, she flopped backward and moved her arms up and down. Then she bounced to her feet and grinned at him. "See? We're angels!"

Snow angels. Noah's throat felt suddenly thick. He leaned on his crutches, grateful for their support.

Still grinning, dripping snow, Susannah hurried toward him, holding out her hand. "Come and make angels."

He didn't move. Couldn't.

"Or maybe you can't," she said, her face suddenly crumpling into a worried frown as she reached him. "Because of your leg?"

He gave himself a little shake. "It's all right."

"You don't have to fall over like we did," she said. "You could lie down careful like. Here. I'll help you." She took his hand.

Oh God. He swallowed painfully as he felt her mittened fingers wrap around his, and he allowed himself to be led. Susannah drew him with her to an pristine patch of untrampled snow next to the small angel she had made.

"Turn around," she directed.

He turned.

"Can you sit down?"

Awkwardly, he did. Then he stretched out full length in the cold snow and, as she watched him, moved his arms slowly up and down at his sides, making the wings. His eyes felt suddenly wet. From the cold, he assured himself.

Not because he was remembering another Christmas. Another pair of angels.

He'd been barely four that Christmas. And lonely, because that was the first year both his older brothers were in school all day. Even six-year-old Luke had left on the school bus each morning and didn't get home until it was nearly dark, so Noah spent the days by himself.

They didn't live in the city, but in an old, two-story tin-roofed ranch house on a remote Colorado mountainside, so he'd had no one to play with. No one to run and wrestle in the snow with. No one to throw snowballs with. Except his mother, who always had plenty of work to do—laundry, cleaning, cooking. Helping his father clean tack, mucking out the barn and doing something she called "book work" that was just columns of numbers to a four-year-old boy. It didn't look interesting at all. Certainly not as interesting as the snow that had begun to fall that morning right after his brothers had gone to school.

Noah had played outside by himself in it until his nose was frozen and his lips were blue. But playing alone was no fun.

"Come out," he'd begged his mother. "Just for a little while."

She'd hesitated, then looked at his pleading face and set aside the ledger with its columns of numbers that never added up the way she wanted them to. She came outside with him and threw snowballs and made a snowman and did all the rough-and-tumble things he did with his brothers. And then she walked over to the one area he hadn't run through, a space of pure, smooth, soft snow.

"Let's make angels," she'd said.

Noah had stared. "Angels?"

"Like this." Her dark hair had curled against her wind-reddened cheeks as she'd smiled down at him. "Watch."

Then, as he'd stared in openmouthed astonishment, his normally serious mother had toppled right over backward and flapped her arms. He'd never seen her do anything so amazing and he'd laughed.

She'd laughed, too. "Come and make an angel, Noah," she'd said as she got up carefully so as not to disturb the shape she'd made in the snow.

And he had. He'd flung himself backward the same way she had, and then, as she watched him, he'd moved his arms, feeling as if he were flying in slow motion through the soft, snowy drifts. And then she'd reached out and pulled him to his feet, then picked him up in her arms and snuggled him close.

"See?" she'd said, smiling and rubbing her nose against his cold cheek. "We're angels."

That was the last Christmas he'd had with his mother. Five months later she'd died in a car accident.

It was the first time he'd let himself think about snow angels in years.

Tess was making more cookies—gingerbread this time—when they came in. The house was filled with the smell of cinnamon and nutmeg, allspice and ginger. It made Noah's mouth water and his stomach growl. And like the snow angels, the memory of that smell made his throat tighten and something deep inside his chest begin once more to ache.

Still, he couldn't ache for long. Once she'd shed her jacket, mittens, hat and boots, Susannah was tugging his hand and looking up at him in bright anticipation. "All ready to make cookies?"

Tess, calm now, looked up and said, "Wash your hands," to Susannah and Libby and, Noah supposed, to him. "There are aprons in the drawer."

Before Noah knew it, he, Susannah and Libby were all wearing aprons. After he rolled out the dough, they cut out reindeer and Santas and Christmas trees and angels. Then

Tess put the cookie sheets into the oven. In the background, songs from Christmases past played on the stereo. But little girls of Christmas present sang along off-key, and Noah, bemused, shared a grin over their heads with Tess.

It was the first genuine grin he'd seen on her face in eight years. The sight caused his heart to lurch oddly against the wall of his chest.

When they were almost finished, there was a knock on the back door. Tess opened it to a windblown-looking woman in her early thirties.

"Mom," Libby crowed, "did you see our angels in the yard?"

The woman nodded. "Hope she hasn't been too much trouble," she said to Tess. Then she saw Noah and her eyes widened. She looked at Tess for an introduction.

Tess hesitated, then said to Noah, "This is Janna. Janna, this is Noah."

She hesitated again, long enough for Susannah to add, "My dad."

Janna blinked, then mustered a polite smile and held out a hand. "How nice to meet you." There was a wealth of meaning in every word.

Noah smiled wryly as he shook her hand. "It's nice to meet you, too."

"Well," Janna said, clearly flustered. "I never expected ... I mean, Tess didn't say you were coming."

"She didn't know," Susannah said matter-of-factly. "I prayed for him."

Janna couldn't seem to think of any response to that. She looked from father to daughter to mother, then at last at her own daughter before she finally decided on an appropriate response.

"Well, good," she said heartily. "Come on, Lib. Get your jacket so we can let Tess and Susannah and—and Noah have the rest of the afternoon to themselves."

Libby groaned. "Aw, Mom. I—"

"Now." Janna's tone brooked no argument. Libby sighed, climbed down off the chair and went to get her jacket. "Maybe I can come back later," she said to Susannah.

Janna chivied her daughter toward the door, shooting a glance back at Tess as she went. "Sorry," Noah heard her say under her breath. "You should have told me. I could have taken her with me."

"Nonsense. It was fine. This was just a fluke."

"He isn't here for Christmas?" Janna asked doubtfully.

"Yes, he is," Susannah said firmly, overhearing the conversation.

"Yes." Noah heard Tess agree. "But he's not staying."

Tess had grown up with the adage "Be careful what you pray for, for you will likely get it." She hadn't realized it applied to one's children's prayers, too. Surely she had never offered up such prayers herself, asking the Almighty for Noah to be a part of their Christmas celebration! Or if she had, it must have been years ago.

Shouldn't there be a statute of limitations on prayers? And shouldn't the one on those particular prayers have long ago run out?

It seemed not. And Tess couldn't help the bittersweet feelings that swept over her whenever she stepped back and allowed herself to acknowledge what was happening that afternoon.

They were making memories. The three of them this time, instead of just two. Memories of snow angels and Christmas baking, of girlish giggles and hearty masculine laughter, of smiles and snowball fights, of tickling and teasing.

It was as if a scene by Norman Rockwell had somehow made it into a Norman Mailer book. Or, if her life wasn't quite that gritty, Tess hedged, at least into a book with a somewhat-harder edge. She reminded herself that it was no more than she'd told Janna it was—a fluke. A brief flash of something special—like those two weeks she and Noah had spent together eight years before. It wouldn't last.

She tried to resist. But Tess had never been a Scrooge. She couldn't say, "Bah, humbug," even when it was clearly in the best interests of her own emotional well-being to do so. No, not her. She was a sap. Altogether too willing to let herself be swept up in the spirit of the season—peace on earth and goodwill to men. Even to the one man she had the most to fear from.

"Just so you remember that," she muttered to herself as she carried a plateful of decorated cookies into the living room so Noah and Susannah could hang them on the tree.

"What?" Noah looked over at her.

She shook her head, unaware until that moment that she'd spoken aloud. "Nothing," she said.

He gave her a searching look, but when she determinedly shook her head again, he turned back to Susannah.

"You tie the loops," she was telling him, "after Mom threads 'em through."

"Loops? Thread? Seems like a lot of work to go through just to eat them," Noah said.

"We don't eat 'em, silly." Susannah giggled. "We hang 'em on the tree."

Noah feigned astonishment. "I've never heard of such a thing," he said.

And Susannah giggled again. "Show him, Mommy."

So Tess threaded a needle and made a hole through the top of each cookie. Then she cut the thread, and under Susannah's tutelage, Noah tied a loop through each one. Then Susannah took them and hung them on the tree. Except on the branches that were too high for her reach.

"See," Tess said as she struggled on tiptoe to put a silver-studded angel on one of the higher branches, "if we'd gotten a short tree, you'd be able to reach."

Susannah shook her head stubbornly. "I like this one. Noah can lift me up. Can't you?"

"Sure." He nodded and held out his arms.

"Your elbow!" Tess protested instinctively. "Your shoulder!"

But Noah lifted Susannah easily, and she turned her head, her dark hair brushing his cheek as she grinned at her mother. "See?" she said. Then she twisted to reach out and hang an angel on the tree. "Mommy, hand me another. Please?" she added when Tess gave her an arch look.

Tess handed her another. And then another, as Noah lifted her first on one side and then on the other until at last all the cookies were in place on the tree.

"There," Susannah said with a satisfied sigh. She gave Noah a hug and then wiggled to the floor. He let her down easily, but as he straightened, Tess saw him wince, then rub his elbow when he thought no one was looking.

Susannah took hold of his hand—as if she couldn't bear not to touch him, Tess realized with an aching feeling somewhere in her midsection. The little girl contemplated the tree with its tiny, colored lights reflected in the shiny icing on the cookies. Then she looked up at her father. "Isn't it beautiful?"

And he looked down at her. "Beautiful," he said softly, and Tess was almost certain he wasn't talking about the tree.

"Did you ever have a tree this pretty before?" Susannah asked.

He shook his head.

"What was the prettiest tree you ever had?"

Noah shifted from one foot to the other. He looked almost at a loss for a moment, then slightly wistful. "Prob'ly the one we had when I was—when I was four," he said at last.

Susannah tugged his hand, pulling him toward the couch. "Tell me about it."

Tess could see his reluctance and felt an urge to jump in and save him, to tell Susannah to mind her own business. But then she thought, *It is her business. He's her father. She has a right to ask.*

Noah settled onto the couch, and Susannah tucked herself beneath his arm, snuggling against him. "Not much to tell," he said finally. "It was just a tree. My dad and my oldest brother cut it and—"

"They cut it?" Susannah was awed. "Really cut it?"

"It's what you do out there. We lived on a ranch. There were a lot of trees. We cut one every year."

"But if you did it every year, why was that one special?"

"Susannah," Tess warned softly. She couldn't help it.

Noah glanced up at her. "It's all right," he said. Then he looked back at Susannah. "It was the last year my mother was alive."

Susannah turned her head and looked up at him. "She died when you were just four?"

He nodded.

Her small hand crept onto his thigh and clasped his big one tightly. "You must've missed her just awful."

He looked down at their clasped hands and gave her a faint smile. "I did. I don't think I ever liked Christmas much after that," he said reflectively. "It seemed sort of hollow. As if the center was gone." Then he looked at her. "Until now."

Tess sucked in her breath.

"What was she like, my grandmother?" Susannah asked him.

"Your grandmother?" He looked puzzled, then the realization hit. "Oh, you mean my mother." There was another smile, this one bemused, almost. "Your grandmother." He repeated the words softly. "She would have liked you a lot."

It was surprisingly easy to talk about his mother then. Memories Noah had tucked away so many years ago that he couldn't believe they were still so close at hand came back unbidden. Maybe it was the season, maybe it was the mood, maybe it was the little girl sitting snugly against him, looking up at him with wide eyes, or maybe—just maybe—it was her mother, who hesitated, hovered, then came to sit in the old oak rocker by the sofa to listen to him.

Whatever it was, it made him open up the past in a way he'd never opened it up before. And if his voice got to sounding a little rusty, and once or twice he had to clear his throat, well, Susannah didn't seem to notice.

And Tess?

Tess didn't say a word, but he was aware every instant of her presence as she sat there, rocking slightly, listening to what he said.

He'd never told her any of this—had never really spoken of his family at all when he'd been with her eight years before. Then it hadn't mattered—or he'd thought it hadn't. Now he knew it did.

No matter how long he'd turned his back on those memories, they were still there. They still mattered. His mother, his father, his brothers—all of them mattered. Family mattered.

Were he and Tess and Susannah a family?

He flicked a glance in Tess's direction. He didn't imagine she'd think so. He suspected she'd deny it in a second.

But whether she wanted to admit it or not, Noah thought he could argue that they were. And they were making memories together this Christmas.

And next Christmas? What about that?

His arm tightened slightly around the narrow shoulders of his daughter. He dropped a kiss on the top of her dark hair. Next Christmas, too, he promised himself.

There was nothing that said he couldn't come back.

That evening he was on the sofa again, reading Susannah a story, while Tess was in the kitchen baking loaves of cranberry bread to give to the neighbors and to Susannah's teacher. When he heard a knock on the back door, Noah assumed it was Libby coming to play again. He heard Tess say something, and he sat up a little straighter when the voice he heard in reply was deep and undeniably masculine.

"Who's that?" he asked Susannah.

Before she could answer, Tess came into the living room, followed by a tall, lean man in a policeman's uniform. Susannah bounced up.

"Hi, Steve!"

"This is Steve Williams, Janna's husband," Tess said calmly, ignoring Noah's scowl. "He stopped to invite us over for dinner tomorrow. This is Susannah's father, Noah Tanner."

He could have stayed on the couch where he was; his bad knee gave him enough of an excuse. But for all that Steve Williams had a wife, he was standing too damn close to

Tess. And if that wasn't enough, the assessing look in his eyes had Noah hauling himself to his feet so he could meet the other man's gaze head-on.

Steve was a inch or so taller and broader shouldered than he was. Even so, Noah figured he could take him in a fight. Unconsciously he flexed his fingers, then curled them into fists. Tess saw the movement and stepped between them, giving him a hard look.

Noah took a deep breath and held out a hand. "Howdy."

Steve's handshake was as firm and no-nonsense as his gaze was unblinking. He dropped Noah's hand almost at once and turned back to Tess. "Janna and I thought, since you were with us last year and the year before, that it's become something of a tradition." He was looking at Tess, though it was clear enough to Noah who he was really talking to. "You're all welcome," he added almost reluctantly.

Tess hesitated.

"We'll be there," Noah said. And if he put just a little more emphasis on the *we* than was strictly necessary, well, he didn't think Steve Williams misunderstood. Their eyes met.

Steve nodded. "Five o'clock." He started for the door, then turned back. "We'll see you in the morning," he said to Susannah.

"Susannah is staying with them while I'm at work," Tess told Noah.

"I can watch her."

Noah saw Tess and Steve exchange glances. "We've already arranged..." Tess began, then stopped when she saw the sudden smile on Susannah's face begin to fade. "Well, I suppose. Are you sure?"

Noah bristled. "Of course I'm sure."

"What about your therapy?"

"It's only an hour. We'll work it out." He winked at Susannah. "Won't we?"

She nodded emphatically, the smile back in place.

Steve was looking sceptical. Tess was looking torn. Finally she sighed. "If you think you can manage."

"We can manage."

"Uh-huh," Susannah echoed. She smiled up at Noah, then leaned against him. He rested a hand on her shoulder and squeezed it lightly.

Steve hesitated, then said mildly, "Well, we'll be there if you wear out."

"I won't."

"It's a little longer than an eight-second ride," Steve pointed out smoothly.

Noah heard Tess suck in her breath. His own spine stiffened. "We'll see you tomorrow night."

Tess laid a hand on Steve's arm and seemed to steer him toward the door. "Five o'clock?"

Steve's gaze never left Noah's, but he allowed himself to be maneuvered back into the kitchen. "That's what Janna said."

Noah waited until Susannah was in bed before he tackled the issue. "Little bit of a watchdog, isn't he?"

Tess, busy wrapping loaves of bread in foil and putting ribbon and bows on them, didn't look up, but she didn't pretend not to know what he was talking about, either. "He and Janna are concerned."

"Janna didn't bite my wrist."

"She sent Steve," Tess said simply. She cut another piece of ribbon and put it around one of the loaves.

Noah shifted against the cabinet he was leaning on. "That's all it is?"

Her head came up abruptly and she gave him a hard look. "All what is?"

"He acts like he owns you."

"He's got a wife."

"That doesn't stop some men."

"It stops Steve. He's never looked at me twice. He's a friend, Noah. In fact, I think it would be fair to say that he and Janna are just about the best friends I've ever had. They've done a lot for Susannah and me since we moved next door. Not just baby-sitting, though heaven knows they've done plenty of that. When Susannah had pneumonia and I couldn't get off work everyday, Steve and Janna took care of her. When she broke her arm, Steve was the one who took her to the hospital. When she needed a 'dad' to go to a Brownies' dinner, he went. They've taken her with them when they've gone camping in the summer and skiing in the winter. I don't know what I would have done without them!" She stopped suddenly, apparently aware that her voice had risen and her fists were clenched.

"I see." He saw a lot more than he wanted to, in fact. Saw that there had been plenty of times when Tess hadn't coped as well as she wanted to give the impression that she had. That there were, whether she liked it or not, circumstances where just one parent wasn't quite enough. Mostly he saw that while he'd been oblivious to everyone's needs but his own, Steve and Janna Williams had been there for Tess and Susannah.

But I didn't know! he thought desperately. But he'd never wanted to know, either.

He'd never felt for any girl what he'd felt for Tess those two weeks they'd been together. It had seemed too serious, too real, too demanding for a man who was, he had to admit, little more than a boy deep down.

If he had stayed, he wouldn't have been much good to
her. He remembered his brother Tanner, who had married
his high-school sweetheart, Clare, when he found out she
was pregnant. Tanner had tried—hell, he'd done everything he could—to be a husband, a father-to-be and the sole
guardian of his two younger brothers. It hadn't worked.

If Tanner couldn't do it, Noah knew there was no way he
could have. He'd been wicked and wild and woolly in those
days. Not much good even to himself.

And now?

"Don't you harass Steve tomorrow night," Tess said, her
tone and her words jerking him back to the moment.

"I won't."

"I mean it." She was clearly unconvinced by his sudden
acquiescence.

He shut his eyes briefly, considering Steve Williams, who
was apparently a good husband, a good father. What was
it Steve Williams had that he lacked?

Noah opened his eyes again and met hers. "I mean it,
too," he said quietly. "I reckon I owe him a ton."

Six

He couldn't sleep. He lay in Tess's bed, tossing and turning, his mind tempted not by visions of seasonal sugarplums, but by photos of a little girl—and a bigger one—that danced through his head.

He'd asked for it, of course. He'd been thinking about all the things Steve Williams had shared with his daughter, and after Susannah had gone to bed, Noah had said to Tess, "Do you have pictures?"

She'd gone to the bookcase next to the fireplace, taken out half a dozen photo albums, and handed them to him. He'd sat on the sofa, turning the pages slowly, watching the years go past. In those few albums he'd caught a glimpse of Tess and Susannah's life for the last seven years. It had made him smile, made him laugh, made him ache.

Tess had left him to look at them alone, disappearing into the kitchen and rattling pots and pans.

"Who's this?" he'd called after her. "Where were you when this happened?"

And after she'd come back a few times to reply, she stayed, first standing beside the sofa, then perching on its arm, then finally sitting next to him and taking the albums in her lap. She'd answered his questions briefly at first. Then, as she looked over the pictures again, she smiled reminiscently and spoke at length.

He heard about holidays and vacations, about nursery school and class field trips and visits from the Easter Bunny. He heard about swimming classes and Brownie plays, horseback riding and Girl Scout Cookie sales.

Tess's voice had been soft and slightly husky. She didn't even try to hide the love and pride she felt. And sometimes, when she choked up a bit as she remembered a particular event, he'd wanted to reach for her hand or slip an arm behind her and pull her close.

He didn't, because he knew any such action would make her stiffen and pull away, and he didn't want to break the spell. So he'd stayed where he was—millimeters from her—until they'd closed the last page and sat silently, side by side, each caught in a tangled web of reflections. And then, just when he'd thought he might dare to turn and touch his lips to hers, Tess slapped her hands lightly on top of the last album and sprang to her feet.

"Well, there you have it," she said briskly. "Seven years in a nutshell. Now, if you don't mind, you're sitting on my resting place and I have to get up at 5:30...."

The moment lost, Noah hauled himself awkwardly to his feet. "I'll sleep out here."

"No. It's easier this way. Then I won't bother you when I leave for work."

He hadn't argued. And when she even declined his help in making up the sofa into a bed, he'd gone meekly off to bed himself.

But not to sleep.

He'd been lying awake for hours, thinking about Susannah—and about Tess. About the years they'd had together. Without him.

A jumble of images somersaulted in his mind, teasing him—a photo of a day-old infant in a pale pink sleeper looking cross-eyed at the camera; a half-dozen shots of a dark-haired toddler with toys and blocks, beside a wading pool or a Christmas tree; glimpses of mother and child at various ages and in various locations, laughing, giggling, mugging for the camera; and one separate section begun three years before, of Susannah smiling for school pictures.

But more than any of those, one particular image haunted him—a slightly blurred shot of Tess on the last page of an album, taken by Susannah. She'd been standing by the Ferris wheel on the midway at the rodeo in Cheyenne.

Had it been taken the day they'd seen him with Maggie?

When he saw it, he'd wanted to ask. He couldn't. Tess had shut the album abruptly, then stood up, effectively putting the past away.

But Noah couldn't.

He got up and, as quietly as he could, made his way out of the room and down the short hall to Susannah's bedroom. The door was slightly ajar and he pushed it open.

The blinds were only half-closed, admitting enough reflected light off the snow so that he could see his daughter snuggled against her pillows, one arm around a stuffed horse. His gaze flicked from Susannah to the pictures of him on her bedside table.

There were none in the photo albums—no sign of him during his daughter's first seven years. Because, of course, he hadn't been here.

But he had to admit that Tess hadn't shut him out of Susannah's life completely. On the contrary, she'd given her daughter as much of her father as she dared. He thanked her for that, even as he knew that it hadn't been enough for Susannah.

It wasn't enough for him, either. He wanted more—of both of them.

Gently he brushed his hand over Susannah's dark hair. She stirred slightly. "M' Chris'mas," she muttered.

Noah's fingers touched her lips, then brushed her hair once more. "Merry Christmas, sweetheart," he whispered. Then he limped out as silently as he'd come.

Downstairs, a soft glow beckoned. Tess had sent him off so she could sleep. So why was a light still on?

He made his way down the steps, and saw that the light came not from the reading lamp by the rocker, but from the Christmas tree. In the golden glow of the myriad tiny, colored lights, Noah could see Tess asleep on the couch.

He moved closer, drawn by the sight of her. She lay on her side, one hand tucked under her head, the other curled into the blanket, clutching it against her chest. Her lips were slightly parted, her hair loose and free against the pillow.

Only once before did he remember watching her sleep. It had been on the morning of the day he'd left, eight years ago. They had loved far into the night, eager and hungry for each other, giving and taking, touching and tasting, until at last, sated, they'd fallen asleep in each other's arms.

Tess had still been sleeping soundly when Noah awoke at the first hint of dawn. He'd lain there, savoring the warmth of her body next to his, already regretting that he wouldn't be enjoying that warmth the next time he went to bed. He'd turned his head and dropped a kiss on her hair, breathing deeply, savoring the soft, flowery scent of her, storing it away. Then he'd eased back, but only far enough to get a good look at her, to have another memory. He remembered thinking how beautiful she was.

He'd never told her that. Never told her, either, that those two weeks eight years ago had been the best two weeks of his life.

Why not?

Because if he had, he might've had second thoughts about what he was doing. And in those days, the only thing that kept him going was focusing on the next town, the next rodeo, the next ride. If he'd allowed himself to get sidetracked, he'd never have succeeded. He'd never have been champion of the world.

He'd have been a husband and a father instead.

A fair trade-off?

Not a fair question; he knew that even as he asked himself. There was no answer to the past. There was only the future.

A future with Tess?

Eight years ago he'd watched her sleep, then he'd taken a deep breath and turned away.

Now he came closer, bending down. She shifted and sighed, but didn't wake. Asleep, she hardly looked older than Susannah. But regardless of how she looked, she was a woman now.

She'd succeeded, too, probably even better than he had—though he certainly had more notoriety. She'd become a nurse. She'd become a mother. She'd raised, single-handedly and well, a beautiful child. His child.

He reached out a hand and touched Tess's hair, the way he had Susannah's. It wasn't enough. He knelt and dropped a kiss on her mouth. Her lips parted at his touch.

He wanted to touch them again. And again. Dropping his head, he rested his forehead lightly against hers. "Thank you," he whispered.

She didn't stir.

Then he got slowly to his feet, adjusted the quilt around her shoulders and shut off the Christmas lights.

He didn't fall sleep until well past four.

"What's wrong?" Janna asked the minute she heard Tess's voice on the phone.

"Nothing," Tess said quickly. She shouldn't have called. Just because she was feeling jittery was no reason to bother Janna. "I just wanted to make sure you knew that Suse was staying with Noah today."

"Steve told me," Janna said. "Is it all right?"

"Of course," Tess said quickly. Too quickly.

"I'll keep an eye out," Janna offered. "I'll take her if you want."

"No. It's all right. I think he'll be fine with her. It's just that . . . just that—"

"Maybe you're worried he'll be too fine with her," Janna said with her usual perception. "And then where will you be?"

"Nowhere," Tess said firmly. "Susannah knows that. She has him for now. Not for always."

"Are you sure?"

"He hasn't given me any reason to think otherwise."

"What would you do if he did?"

Tess didn't want to think about that. "He won't," she said. "I've got to go. But, yes, keep an eye out, would you? Just in case . . ."

"No problem," Janna said. "I'm sure Libby will want to play with Susannah. He won't even know I'm checking."

"Good. He'll think I don't trust him otherwise."

"Do you?"

"Yes, oddly enough." With Susannah, at least. She had seen it in him from the very first, that intense concern about their daughter, that desire to keep her safe. He had the right instincts where fatherhood was concerned, Tess thought.

"I've got to go," she said again. There was absolutely no future in thinking things like that.

Someone was standing over him.

Noah could sense it at once, even without opening his eyes. The force of a stare, the shallow, quick intake of breath brought him through grogginess to full alert. How long had he been out? What horse had flattened him? His eyes snapped open.

"Good. You're awake."

Noah sagged back against the pillow, the rodeo arena of his dreams fading, the reality of Susannah staring him in the face.

"Morning," he mumbled, scrubbing a hand over his eyes, then squinting at her. "What time is it?"

"Seven," his daughter said cheerfully.

Noah stifled a groan. The last time he'd seen seven o'clock willingly, he had come at it from the other end.

"I brought you breakfast in bed."

"Breakfast? In bed?" He didn't think he'd ever had breakfast in bed in his life—not unless you counted potato chips and a six-pack of beer.

But Susannah was bending down and picking up the tray on the floor beside her. "It's not much. Cheerios and toast and orange juice. Mom won't let me use the stove unless she's here," she confided as she stood waiting expectantly for him to sit up.

Noah shoved himself up against the pillows. She settled the tray on his lap and handed him a napkin. He took it, then contemplated the very crisp toast and the slightly soggy cereal, and rubbed a hand across his whiskered jaw.

"Is it okay?" she asked nervously.

"It's wonderful," he told her. "No one has ever done this for me before."

"Never?" Her surprise showed. "Mom does it for me on my birthday every year. An' last year I did it for her on Mother's Day. I know it isn't Father's Day, but ... you're prob'ly not gonna be here then," she said with determined indifference, and Noah felt a sudden twist in his gut at the assumption. "So I thought I'd do it now."

"It's the nicest thing you could have done."

Under Susannah's watchful eye, he ate every bite. Then while she carried the dishes back down to the kitchen, Noah pulled on a clean pair of jeans and buttoned a blue plaid flannel shirt across his chest. He was pulling on his boot when Susannah reappeared.

"What shall we do now?" she asked.

"How about you give me a hand making this bed," he said. "Then I'll help you with yours. And then, well ... we'll see."

He'd expected Tess to leave him instructions, but apparently she hadn't. Still, his suggestion seemed to be the right one. "Mommy always says we have to get the house ready for Christmas, too," Susannah told him. "We can do it and surprise her."

So they made beds together. They did a load of laundry together. Then Noah washed the breakfast dishes while Susannah dried them. Afterward Susannah dusted the furniture and Noah vacuumed the carpet and swept the floors.

Then he said, "Coffee break," and made them both cups of cocoa, which he carried into the living room.

"Are you sure?" Susannah said doubtfully. "Mom doesn't let me drink out here."

"It's a special occasion," Noah decided. "We'll both be careful."

And they sat in the living room, side by side on the sofa, listening to a tape of holiday music that Noah put on. Susannah sipped her cocoa, then looked up at him and smiled shyly.

"I'm glad I asked God for you to come," she told him. "You're better'n a Barbie doll."

Noah was glad to hear that. He contemplated the clean house, the well-lit Christmas tree, the fire now crackling in the fireplace, the cat curled on the hearth rug, the small girl sitting next to him, and he felt a lump growing in his throat.

He said, "I'm glad you asked God, too."

If the day before had brought Noah all kinds of memories, today was a whole new experience.

He'd never been a parent before. Not really. The night he'd gone with Tess and Susannah to buy the tree, and yesterday, with Tess home to give orders and make decisions, didn't count. She'd been the parent then and he'd been hanging around.

Today, for the first time in his life, Noah felt the sense of being responsible for another person begin to settle in on him.

Susannah looked to him for answers, decisions, permission. He decided they'd clean the house. He decided they'd take a break. He decided they could drink cocoa in the living room.

It was heady stuff.

He felt benevolent and in charge when, shortly before noon, he let his daughter go out to play with Libby and her ten-year-old brother, Jeff.

"Half an hour," he said. "Then we'll go Christmas shopping."

He watched her trot down the steps, then he made himself a cup of coffee and settled down to read yesterday's paper and enjoy fatherhood.

Ten minutes later Jeff was banging on the back door. "Susannah's bleeding!"

What Noah said then was more instinctual than fatherly. He pushed past Jeff and hobbled, crutchless, out into the yard. She wasn't there! He spun around toward the boy. "Where is she? What happened?"

"Down the street in Radloffs' backyard. We were swingin' each other around and lettin' go and—"

"Show me!"

The wind cut through the thin flannel of his shirt as he limped hurriedly after Jeff. His leg ached and his teeth were chattering by the time Jeff turned into a driveway. Noah didn't notice anything but Susannah.

She was huddled on the ground, with Libby and two children Noah didn't know hovering around her. He pushed past them and crouched down as best he could.

His daughter looked up at him with an abraded cheek, a bloody nose, a split lip and one front tooth missing. Tears were drying on her cheeks, but he could see her striving to keep her voice from wobbling when she spoke. "I hit a tree."

Oh God, Noah thought. And the next thing he thought was, *Oh, Tess!*

He couldn't count how many times he'd scraped Taggart and dozens of other buddies up off the dirt in the arena when they'd been stomped by some of the rankest rough stock around. He did it as a matter of course and never batted an eye.

Now he couldn't move, couldn't think. He wanted Tess. He needed Tess!

A parent would know what to do!

And then he realized that he was the parent here. He swallowed his panic and tried to think.

Susannah wasn't dying. She was cut. She was bleeding. She was missing a tooth. "Is it just your face?" he asked her. "I mean, do you hurt anywhere else?"

She shook her head slightly, then grimaced. "Ow."

"How hard did you hit?" Did she have a concussion? He peered at her pupils. They looked all right. "Who are you?"

She giggled slightly. "You know that." She shot a glance at Libby and rolled her eyes.

"I do? That's right, I do," Noah said, snapping his fingers as if it had just come back to him. "You're Abigail."

Another giggle. "No, thilly. I'm Thuthannah."

Noah winced.

Susannah, hearing herself, giggled again. "Thuthannah," she repeated, carefully poking her tongue against her lip through the gap where her tooth had been.

So she didn't have a concussion. Just a new lisp, he thought grimly. And he was getting his wits back slowly—wit by wit, it seemed. "And you're five?" he persisted, just to make sure.

"Theven," she corrected.

"Right. Seven." He groped in his pocket for a handkerchief to hold to her nose. The blood seemed to be stopping anyway, probably because of the cold. "See if you can find her tooth," he said to the children. He remembered Deke Miller getting his front teeth hammered by a bull a few years back in Scottsdale. Someone with foresight had taken them along to the dentist, and he'd been able to save them.

They scurried over to the tree—all but Libby, who seemed more concerned about the rest of Susannah. She crouched down next to Noah. "We didn't mean to hurt her," she said earnestly. "We were just playing. Jeff and Terry were swinging us. I went first. Then it was Susannah's turn. Is she going to be okay?'' Her eyes were wide and worried.

"She'll be fine," Noah promised. "Will it hurt if I pick you up, Susannah?"

"D-don't think tho."

"Tell me if it does." He slid his arms under her and gritted his teeth, trying to get enough purchase in the snow-covered grass with his bad leg to stagger upright and not drop her. He stumbled slightly, but made it. Susannah wrapped her arms like iron bands around his neck.

"Got it!" The boy called Terry came running, Susannah's tooth clutched tightly in his fist.

They made an odd procession along the sidewalk, Noah carrying Susannah, Libby and the other girl flanking him on either side, while Jeff ran ahead to open the door and Terry carried the tooth in his clenched fist.

The Williamses' door opened as he passed, and Janna flew out. "What happened? Is she all right? Shall I call Tess?"

"No," Noah said. "Don't call Tess."

Not yet. Please God, don't let her see what a mess I've made of her daughter yet! He stumbled through the gate. Out of the corner of his eye, he could see Janna coming his way. "Go tell your mother she's okay," he told Libby. Then he carried Susannah into the house.

Jeff followed him. "Want me to call 911?"

"No." He set Susannah on the kitchen counter and grabbed a clean dishcloth, then dabbed at her nose and cheek, trying not to grimace and feel faint at the sight of all her blood.

God knew he'd seen plenty in his life. Why this should bother him so much he didn't know—unless it was because it was his daughter's.

"Who's your dentist?" he asked Susannah when he finished.

"Dr. Kincaid," Janna said, and he turned to find her standing right behind him. "I'll ca—I'll get you the number," she said.

The dentist's receptionist said to bring her right in. That was when Noah remembered he didn't have a car.

He borrowed Janna's. "I'll rent one," he promised, "as soon as we finish at the dentist's."

"Don't worry about it," she said, hovering over Susannah as Noah tucked her into the front seat of the car. "Are you sure you don't want me to call Tess? She'd come."

"No. I can handle it," Noah said. His knuckles were white on the steering wheel. He hoped he was telling her the truth.

At least Susannah wasn't crying for her mother. On the contrary, she wasn't crying at all. She sat stoically beside him and didn't say a word while he drove and tried to remember Janna's directions. Every few seconds he slanted a glance down at Susannah and winced at the scrape on her cheek, the blood drying beneath her nose and on her puffy lip.

What kind of father let his kid get smashed to bits the moment he let her out of his sight?

"Bring her right on back, Mr. Montgomery," the dentist's assistant said when he led Susannah into the office. With Susannah clutching his hand, he followed the woman to a room at the end of the hall. "Dr. Kincaid will be right in."

Noah alternated between hovering and pacing until the dentist arrived.

Dr. Kincaid was a short, cheerful man in his fifties. "Smile," he said to Susannah. Then, when she did, "Oh, my."

"We've got the tooth." Noah fished desperately in the pocket of his jeans.

"Open wide," Dr. Kincaid said, and with a gloved finger, he wiggled Susannah's other, intact front tooth.

"Here." Noah thrust the missing tooth at him.

"Give it to the tooth fairy."

"You can't save it?"

Dr. Kincaid glanced up and grinned. "No need. She's got a spare just waiting to come in."

"It was a . . . baby tooth?" Noah almost sagged with relief.

"Not that I would recommend such a drastic procedure for getting rid of your loose teeth every time, young lady," Dr. Kincaid said to Susannah.

She giggled.

"We'll take an X ray to be sure that everything's all right below the gum line. But judging from the looks of the one that's left, the one she knocked out was ready to go."

"Thank God."

Noah wasn't relishing explaining the split lip, bloody nose and scraped face to Tess. But not having to tell her that Susannah was going to go through life a snaggle-toothed wonder made things marginally better. He sagged into the chair and waited while Susannah sat stoically through the X ray. Then Dr. Kincaid cleaned her abrasions once more and bandaged the cut above her lip.

"I don't think she needs stitches," he said. "Just lots of TLC and plenty of soft food. She won't want to be chewing much for a day or so. Maybe you can talk your dad into a big dish of ice cream," he suggested to Susannah.

She looked hopefully at Noah.

He said, "I think that might be arranged."

The doctor helped her out of the chair, then ruffled her hair and winked. "You tell your parents the tooth fairy better give you combat pay for that tooth."

Susannah grinned, then grimaced when the bandage above her lip pulled.

As they were going out the door, she looked up at Noah. "Do you know 'bout the tooth fairy?" she asked a little dubiously.

He smiled. "We've met a time or two."

She sighed. "Good."

They were heading back to Janna's car when Noah noticed that his hands were trembling. He stuffed them in his pockets. *She's all right,* he assured himself. *She's fine.* But it was all he could do not to scoop her up in his arms and just stand there, holding her, while he listened to her breathing. Did all fathers feel this way when bad things happened to their children or was it just the rookies?

"We'll pick up some ice cream on the way home," he promised as they got into the car.

Susannah looked disappointed. "Why can't we just get it when we go Chrithmuth thopping?"

He stared at her. "You want to go shopping?"

"I got to get a prethent for Mom. You thaid we would," she reminded him. "Thith morning."

"That was before you went head-on with a tree. You're sure you feel well enough?"

"Courth," Susannah said. She fastened her seat belt, then looked over at him. "I didn't cry in there at all. I wath tough, wathn't I, Noah? Brave, like you are when you get bucked off?"

Noah, about to back out of the parking place, stopped and looked at his small daughter. She was holding herself very still, her back straight, her hands clenched into tight little fists. Only her eyes wavered uncertainly as she looked at him.

A corner of his mouth tilted. He drew a finger along the curve of her jaw. "You were one tough hombre, Susannah."

Her gaze steadied. She managed a smile, a tiny one that didn't hurt. "Thath's all right, then."

Janna took them to get a rental car, and if she was dismayed at Noah taking Susannah, still bloody but unbowed, Christmas shopping, she didn't say so. She just asked, "We'll still see you for dinner at five?" when she dropped them off at the rental agency.

"We'll be there," Noah promised.

Shopping with Susannah was a painstaking process. For a man who could remember his own boyhood penchant for going through his meager allowance like it was water, watching his daughter comparison shop was something to behold. Obviously she'd got her frugal-consumer gene from her mother.

"I'm getting bubble bath. Mom likes bubble bath," Susannah told him when they'd shopped all the way up and down Third Street, after which she insisted he take her to one of the big discount stores. She was speaking slowly, avoiding the gap where her tooth had been, forming her words, especially the ones with *S* sounds, carefully. "The flowery ones."

"They had bubble bath in the last store."

"Yeah, but it's cheaper at the other place," she explained. "I only have six dollars and twenty-five cents. And I gotta buy you a present, too."

"No, you don't."

Susannah just looked at him. "I do."

It wasn't hard to figure out what to buy Susannah. The only thing she had eyes for was a bike. She didn't say anything when they wandered through the toy section, but her gaze lingered on a shiny red bicycle, and she ran her fingers over the handlebars as they went past.

"Libby has a bike like that," she said.

"Lucky girl," Noah replied. "Though I don't know how she'll ride it in the snow."

"It doesn't matter," Susannah said. "She'll ride it again in the spring." She got a sort of wistful, faraway look in her eyes, and it didn't take a mind reader to see what she was seeing—Libby racing past on her bright red bike, leaving Susannah standing on the curb, watching.

Not if he had anything to say about it!

She helped him pick out toys for Tanner and Maggie's three and Luke and Jill's little one. He bought bubble bath—the kind Susannah recommended—for both of his sisters-in-law. Then they went to a Western outfitter's store, and he bought a bridle for Tanner and a flashy rodeo shirt for Luke.

He didn't know what to get Tess.

"What do you think?" he asked Susannah. "What would your mother like?"

Susannah open her mouth, then seemed to think better of it. Her eyes got a soft, sad look in them as she just glanced at him and shook her head.

Nita LongReach was standing just outside the physical-therapy department when Noah and Susannah walked in. After one look at Susannah, she didn't even notice Noah. "I'll get her mother," she said.

"Don't," Noah said quickly. "She's all right."

Nita glanced at him and did a double-take. "My, aren't you a fast worker."

Noah flushed.

Susannah took his hand. "He's my dad."

Nita's eyes almost popped out of her head. Noah's face burned hotter, but he made himself face her astonished stare.

Finally Nita got control of herself enough to press her lips together. She shook her head. "Oh, my," she said. "Oh, my!"

If she'd wanted to say more, she didn't get a chance, for the nurse from therapy called Noah's name and he went in, taking Susannah with him.

He rode the exercise bike. He lifted weights. He did the treadmill—all under Susannah's watchful eye. And all with the appropriate, macho bravado.

But when the therapist went to bend his knee, Noah's tough-guy image almost flew out the window.

Only the sight of his solemn-faced daughter watching him kept him swallowing his groans. Only the memory of her determined stoicism at the dentist's kept the involuntary tears that lined his eyelids unshed.

He was sweating and shaking when he was done.

"Best yet," the therapist said with an approving grin. "You'll have to bring her along every time."

Noah sagged onto the chair and grunted.

Susannah took a towel and gently wiped beads of sweat off his face. Her expression was serious as she studied him. "You were very brave."

Noah reached out a hand and touched her hair. Then a sound made him look up. Tess was standing in the doorway.

Seven

Obviously Nita had passed along word of their arrival. And if the look on Tess's face was anything to go by, she'd also given her a hint of what to expect.

Noah held his breath.

Tess crossed the room slowly, the only sign of her tension the clenching and unclenching of her fingers. Susannah turned to see who he was looking at, and for the first time, Tess saw her face. Noah tensed, waiting for the accusations to begin.

"Well," she said, letting out a long, slow breath, "at least you didn't break your nose."

Susannah grinned, displaying the gap where her tooth had been. "Th'other one wiggles, too," she said, demonstrating with her tongue.

"So it does," Tess said as she crouched down to Susannah's level to get a closer look.

"I took her to the dentist," Noah offered nervously, still expecting the other shoe to drop. "I took the tooth, too, but he said it was ready to come out."

"It was."

"I didn't mean—I never wanted—" he began desperately.

Tess straightened and met his eyes. Her smile was gentle, almost rueful. "Welcome," she said, "to fatherhood."

He wasn't sure that she didn't expect him to turn tail and run.

Three days ago, if someone had offered it to him, he was damned certain he would have. But now, he felt something inside him settle down and take root.

A sense of fatherhood? A notion of commitment to this child?

Yes.

And to her mother.

The thought came out of nowhere, unbidden, unheralded. And undeniable, for all he wasn't expecting it.

And to her mother? What did that mean?

It meant marry Tess.

Was that what he was thinking? The notion rocked him.

But yes, now that he considered it, that was exactly what he was thinking. Eight years ago he'd shoved away any thoughts of marriage without daring to take even a quick look. The very thought of tying himself to anyone or anything terrified him.

Not anymore.

On the contrary, it was attractive as hell. Hadn't he been moaning to Taggart the very day they'd been hit about being the lone bachelor among his brothers? Hadn't he been coveting their homes and their kids and their marital bliss?

Well, hell, he had a kid. He could have a home.

He could have Tess.

As if she was aware of what was going through his mind at that very moment, he saw a flicker of apprehension cross Tess's face. She looked at him warily. "What?"

He shook his head quickly. He might know his mind at last, but he had enough sense not to spring a proposal on her in the middle of a waiting room.

"I was just thinking I like being a father," he said, when it was clear she was waiting for some sort of answer.

Susannah beamed.

Tess looked at him, then quickly away. "Yes, well... Christmas isn't over yet."

"I think I might like being a father for longer than Christmas."

Susannah's eyes widened. Her jaw dropped.

Tess's mouth pressed into a tight line. "Don't," she said softly, "make promises you won't keep."

Susannah, who'd had her prayers answered, and who had a scraped face and a tantalizing new gap in her grin, was the focus of everyone's attention at the Williamses' dinner. Everyone's attention, that is, except Noah's.

He didn't precisely ignore his daughter. But more than he watched Susannah, he watched Tess.

He watched her smiling as she helped Janna put the food on the table. He watched her bend and give Susannah a gentle kiss on the forehead in the one spot that hadn't been abraded by her collision with the tree. He watched her laughing at Jeff's retelling of Susannah's encounter with the tree—and it was funny, now that she was fine.

But Noah wasn't thinking about that. He was thinking that he wanted those smiles and those kisses and those gentle laughs to be for him.

And the only other thing he was aware of was that, while he was watching Tess, Steve watched him. Narrowly. Speculatively. Assessingly. Not saying much, just watching. Until supper was over, and Janna and Tess and the kids were cleaning up before they all went to a local nursing home to sing carols with Susannah and Libby's Brownie troop.

Then Steve pushed back his chair and said, "Speaking of hunting, you might like to take a look at my guns."

Noah, who knew a cue when he heard one, said, "I wouldn't mind," and followed Steve down the hall to a small den. Jeff hopped up and started to follow them.

"Not now," his father said.

"But—"

Steve stopped in the doorway and gave his son a stern look. "I said not now."

He was probably a good cop, Noah thought. He did authority well. Jeff obviously thought so. The boy sighed and slunk back toward the kitchen.

Steve ushered Noah into the den and shut the door. He went to the tall oak gun cabinet on the far side of the room, took out his key and opened it.

"I'd have let him stay," he said, not looking at Noah, "because I think it's important for a father to teach his son about guns. My father taught me. But..." He gave a slight shrug as his voice trailed off.

"But you wanted to talk about something other than guns."

Steve's eyes met Noah's. He didn't say anything for a moment. Then a corner of his mouth twisted wryly. "And you're going to say it's none of my business."

"Maybe."

"And maybe, in a strict sense, you'd be right," Steve said flatly. "But Tess has been our friend for three years. She's a good friend. We don't want her getting hurt."

"Neither do I."

They stared at each other, neither giving an inch, neither looking away. Finally Steve nodded, apparently satisfied that he'd made his point. He reached into the cabinet and took out a rifle. He put one foot on the seat of a high-back chair and cradled the rifle on his thigh. He ran his hand down the barrel lovingly, his head bent as he studied the stock. Then he lifted his gaze and met Noah's once more. "She's a beauty."

They weren't talking about guns. Noah nodded. "Yes."

"She deserves the best a man has got."

"I know."

"And that little gal—she's as precious to me as my own."

Noah inclined his head. "You've done good by 'em both. I appreciate that."

"Tess said you didn't know about Susannah." Steve balanced the gun in his hands for a long moment, then offered it to Noah.

He took it, letting it rest lightly in his palms, becoming accustomed to the weight. "No. But it's no excuse. I was young and dumb. I didn't think." He shrugged. "I should have known."

A fleeting, rueful smile crossed Steve's face. "I didn't, when Janna was pregnant. And I was with her every day."

Noah stared.

Steve nodded. "Reckon we both were a little too quick on the draw," he said ruefully. He ducked his head momentarily, rocked back on his heels and stuffed his hands in his back pockets. "She told me when she was three months along. And I married her."

"Just like that?"

The grin flickered again. "I had to undergo a bit of an attitude adjustment first. My old man helped. So did hers."

"You plannin' on helpin' me?"

"Do you need it?"

"Nope."

Steve smiled. "Then enough said."

He was watching her. Had been watching her all evening. So what was new about that? Tess thought irritably. He'd been watching her since the moment he opened his eyes and recognized the nurse standing over him.

This wasn't the same.

That had been flirting, teasing, a typical Noah Tanner approach to a woman he wanted to put the make on.

This was something else.

Or maybe she was hallucinating, wanting it to be something else. Because, God help her, she still wanted him. Even though she knew better, even though she knew he was as dependable as a snowman in springtime, she wanted him.

She'd tried not to, for goodness sake. She'd done her absolute best to hold him at arm's length ever since he'd dropped back into her life. But her absolute best didn't seem to be good enough. Not when Noah's deep blue eyes and all the matchmakers in Laramie, Wyoming, were working against her.

There was Susannah, of course. Even though her daughter hadn't actually said anything, Tess was no fool. She knew what Susannah wanted: her mother and her father together at last. So much so that she even gave up her chance next to Noah at the Williamses' dinner table, saying, "Can I sit by Libby? Mom can sit here."

And damned if Janna didn't go along with it. Because drat her, her neighbor seemed to be conspiring against her too.

"He's all right," Janna had said, taking Tess aside when they'd come for dinner. "He handled that business with Susannah's tooth very well."

It was a high compliment from Janna, whose parenting instincts were finely tuned. "He's got what it takes."

Tess hadn't answered. Maybe he did have what it took to be a father; she didn't know. She didn't imagine she'd ever find out, even though Janna and even Steve seemed to think it was a good idea.

So did Nita, who had stopped her as they were leaving work that afternoon. "You're a dark horse," she'd teased. All the nurses had thought so, especially when Susannah didn't hesitate to reveal that Noah wasn't just any old patient who'd dropped in at Tess's house. "Who'd have thought you had a man like that on a string all these years?" Nita grinned.

"I didn't," Tess had protested.

But Nita had laughed. "Not much," she'd said. She meant the opposite.

Her view seemed to be the majority one at the Green Acres Rest Center, too. At least that was the impression Tess got when she and Janna took the girls' Brownie troop there that evening to sing carols.

"You don't have to come," she'd said to Noah firmly.

"I want to," he replied just as firmly.

"I'll come, too," Steve offered. And so they went.

Susannah might have looked like she'd gone ten rounds with the devil, but she sang like an angel. Tess would have beamed as proudly as she always did, if she hadn't been aware of Noah's eyes on her every minute. She wanted to tell him, "Watch the children, not me!" But she knew the guileless, innocent look she'd get if she did. So she suffered in silence. And grew more aware of him by the minute.

She wasn't the only one. Every single person she knew who listened to the Brownies sing that evening—Malcolm and Kenton and Buck, Addie Mae and Trudi, Joyce and Harriet and Sister Saint Joan, all the residents she and Susannah and the Brownie troop had visited during the year—enjoyed the program. But every one of them was far more interested in the man they didn't know, the one who, as Addie said, "had eyes only for Tess."

And when they found out who he was—because, of course, Susannah had to drag him from one to the other after they'd finished singing and say, "This is my father"—well, Tess could see the wheels turning in those elderly heads!

"Ah," they each said with a sigh, and looked him over with such intense interest that if she'd been Noah, she'd have wanted to crawl under a rock.

And then, as if their blatant speculation wasn't enough, each and every one of them shook his hand and said, "It's about time."

Noah seemed to take it all in stride. And Tess was the one who was squirming as his gaze never left her while he said to one and all, "You're right. It is."

And what, she'd like to know, was that supposed to mean?

Damn it, where was all that indifference she'd been so carefully cultivating since the moment Noah Tanner had reappeared in her life? What had happened to her stoic disinterest, her determinedly casual nonchalance in the face of anything he might do?

The longer he looked, the more she felt as if she was on fire.

"My goodness, Tess," Addie Mae said to her as they were leaving, "you have a regular holiday glow."

Which made it even worse.

She was glad that Susannah was almost asleep on her feet by the time they got home. It gave Tess an excuse to slip away from Noah's gaze. "I'll just help her get ready for bed," she said over her shoulder as she hustled her yawning daughter up the stairs.

Unfortunately for her, Susannah cooperated completely, and thirty seconds after her head hit the pillow, she was asleep. The only thing she said to her mother as she nestled beneath the quilt was, "They liked him, didn't they?"

Tess nodded. She couldn't pretend not to know what Susannah meant.

Susannah smiled and hugged her stuffed bear against her chest. "Good," she murmured, her eyes drifting shut. "I thought they would."

Tess stood looking down at her blissfully sleeping daughter, then reached out and smoothed a lock of hair away from her face. "Don't want it," she whispered. "Oh, darling, don't."

It was vain advice and she knew it. But she had to say it because she knew all too well the pain of wanting what she couldn't have.

It was too much to hope that Noah would have taken himself off to bed by the time she got back downstairs. Instead, he was in the kitchen pouring out two cups of tea.

"Tea?" Tess's eyes widened.

"Cowboys drink tea," he said defensively. "My old man drank nothing else. My mother used to make it for us kids, too, sometimes, when we'd had a hard day. 'Cures what ails you,' she used to say."

"And what is ... ailing us?" Tess asked cautiously.

He gave her a wry glance. "I thought maybe seein' your daughter look like she'd plowed the north forty with her face would do it."

"I told you, it happens. Stuff happens ... to kids. You can't prevent it." But she took the tea gratefully when he held it out to her, curling her fingers around the cup, glad that she had it to hide behind. He was looking at her again.

"You were a lot nicer about it than you might've been."
As he spoke, he moved toward the door that led to the living room, herding her before him, so that she found herself on the sofa without really understanding how she got there. He sat down beside her. Close. Very close.

She took a hasty swallow and burned her tongue. "Is that another way of implying you think I can be a bitch?" she asked.

"Hell, no!" His look became as earnest as it was intense. "How can you say that? My word, Tess, you're just about the sweetest gal—you *are* the sweetest gal I've ever known."

It was sweet talk, and she knew it. Sugar-coated words designed to make her soften and smile and welcome him with open arms.

And God help her, she wanted to do just that.

With everything in her she had been resisting him for so long, fighting her attraction to him so hard, that she was worn out. Her defenses were a shambles; the walls she'd tried so desperately to build against him were rubble at her feet. She had no strength left. And she wanted nothing more than to stop fighting him. And herself.

She wanted to reach out. She wanted—fool that she was—to love.

She wasn't quite a big enough fool to believe she'd get it. Not love. Not from a footloose cowboy who, she knew only too well, would be on the road again a few days hence.

But tonight—just tonight—with Noah; yes, she could have that.

As long as she didn't expect undying promises, as long as she knew exactly what she was getting—a night of warmth and comfort, a night of sharing—it would be all right. She would be safe.

Wouldn't she?

Tess didn't examine her reasoning too closely. It wouldn't stand up to scrutiny, as she well knew. But she also knew that she didn't have the energy to resist any longer. She had been without a man's touch—*this man's touch*—far too long. She was only human, after all. She had needs as much as anyone.

It was almost Christmas, so maybe her needs were nearer the surface than usual. Or maybe it was just that Noah was nearer than usual.

Whatever... When he took the cup from her fingers and set it on the coffee table out of the way, she didn't object. And when he set his own down, too, and laid his hands lightly on her arms, she didn't pull away. On the contrary, she found herself leaning into his touch, seeking it, seeking him.

She knew it was foolish. She knew that tomorrow she'd doubtless be sorry. But the light in his deep blue eyes drew her like a moth to a flame.

"Just tonight," she whispered. "Just tonight."

She didn't even think Noah heard. If he did, he paid no attention. As she spoke, his lips came down to swallow her words.

This kiss was different from the one he'd given her in the hospital. That had been a conquest—the kiss of a man with something to prove. This kiss was far gentler, far sweeter, far, far harder to resist.

Not that Tess was in any way resisting. She'd lost that battle. She wasn't even thinking about the war. Her only thoughts were of Noah and the moment. She wanted him— she *needed* him—now.

It was she who deepened the kiss, she who slipped her arms around him and tugged his shirttails out of his jeans. And as he shuddered at the feel of her hands against his heated skin, she smiled.

Yes. Yes. Just for tonight, she could have him.

Take it slow, Noah had told himself. *Go easy.* He hadn't counted on her sweeping him off his feet.

He'd been prepared to work this evening, to soothe and gentle Tess with the same patience his father had used on a skittish mare, to win her around.

But somewhere along the line, patience was no longer an issue, soothing and gentling were beside the point. He wasn't having to draw Tess along with him, he was having to put the brakes on!

If she kept on touching him the way she was, it was going to be over before they'd begun.

She'd touched him in the hospital. She'd held him and helped him and soaped him and washed him, and all the time, she'd treated him with the interest she might show a stick of wood. Her touch might have excited him then, if it hadn't so obviously done nothing for her.

Not so tonight. Not if the tremor in her fingers was anything to go by as they skimmed up beneath his shirt. And if it was affecting her, it was setting him on fire.

His "go easy, take it slow" took on an entirely different meaning once she'd unbuttoned his shirt and eased it off his shoulders, when her fingers began to work on his belt and her lips pressed another kiss on his. The merest brush of her fingers on the denim that covered him and he was in danger of burning right down to the ground!

Not that he was complaining. God, no. But—

"Tess! Wait!"

She stopped abruptly, her eyes wide and worried, her body suddenly stiff. "What? What's wrong?"

"Nothing. Nothing's wrong. It's right." He smiled wryly and leaned toward her to kiss her eyelids. "Too right." With trembling fingers, he worked with slow precision to undo the buttons of her blouse. "I want you bad. But I want it to last. So easy does it, darlin'. We've got all night."

Tess took a deep breath, and he saw a shudder run through her. Her lashes dropped for just a moment, then she nodded and a faintly wistful smile touched her lips. "You're right," she said. "We have all night."

It wasn't enough. It would never be enough; she knew that. But she also knew it was all she was going to get. And so she did her best to simply immerse herself in the moment, to savor the smiles and the touches and the heat of his flesh against hers.

She would have tugged his jeans off right there on the sofa, but he wouldn't let her. "No," he said in a ragged whisper. "Not here." And he drew her to her feet and up the stairs.

She should have protested. She didn't want him making love to her in her bedroom. When the night was over, when Christmas had come and gone—and so had Noah—she didn't want to have to face the memory every day. But even so, she seemed powerless to resist. And when he ushered her into her room and eased the door shut behind them, she pulled back the covers and welcomed him into her arms.

It felt like coming home. She had forgotten how pleasurable the warm, solid weight of his body pressing into hers really was. No, that wasn't true. She'd never forgotten. She had only tried to.

There had been other men in her life in the eight years after Noah. There had been no other men in her bed.

She had tried to become interested in some of them: Mark the respiratory therapist and Steven, the CPA. She hadn't lacked for men who were interested in her. But none of them had attracted her in the least. Like Derek Mallon, they were pleasant and kind, but they weren't Noah.

Noah. After all these years. Tears pricked behind her
eyelids as she felt the rough brush of his whiskers against her
chin. Noah. A lump formed in her throat as his callused
fingers caressed the smooth skin of her breasts. Noah. A fire
rose within her as he moved to slip her jeans and panties
down her hips.

Heaven help her, she still loved him.

And he was loving her. Not the way she loved him, but the
only way he knew how. With his lips and his body, with the
sure, gentle touch of his hands.

Tess gave herself over to it, allowing herself to relish what
he could give, and giving to him in return. She had waited
so long; she had so much to share. But she heeded his words
and took her time.

They had all night.

She wouldn't think about the morning.

Noah hadn't been celibate since he'd made love with Tess.
But he'd never had a woman who could hold a candle to her.
No other woman had ever welcomed him into her bed, into
her arms, into her body, the way Tess did. No other woman
had made him feel so cherished, so valued, so loved.

He'd been a fool not to see it eight years before. But he
wasn't a fool any longer. She was everything he wanted in a
woman. And he set about with all the skill he possessed to
show her.

It wasn't easy. He wanted her desperately. He made himself slow down. He shed his jeans and shorts and lay beside
her on the bed. With his hand, he smoothed the curves of
her body, then leaned in to touch his lips to hers. He made
himself linger over her lips, her breasts, the smooth, shapely
length of her legs. He savored the petal softness of her skin,
so different from his own, taking his time, taking his plea-
sure—and hers—before at last his fingers found the center
of her.

"Noah!" She stiffened and then melted at his touch.

"Mmm." He smiled, pressing a kiss to her lips as he slid between her thighs. "Not ready yet?"

"I'm ready!" Her legs came around him, drawing him in.

She was so tight and wet and warm that he very nearly lost it right then. Only the fact that she held perfectly still—held *him* perfectly still—saved him. He caught his breath. Then, when he dared, he at last began to move.

She tried to go easy. She tried to take it slow. But she'd waited so long—*years!*—for him. Her careful composure deserted her; her control snapped. She moved with him, at first as slowly as she was sure he wanted; but then, because she couldn't help it, the tempo picked up. She moved faster, harder, more desperately.

"Noah!" She gasped his name against his shoulder. Her fingernails dug into his back. Her body convulsed around him. She wept.

It wasn't slow. It wasn't easy. It shattered him. *She* shattered him. He tasted tears on her cheeks and didn't know whether they were hers or his own. Then he spent himself deep within her and sank exhausted, replete, content at last, into the cradle of her arms.

They'd had all night.

They'd loved—quickly and desperately, slowly and languorously, sweetly and playfully. And then, not long before morning, they'd slept.

Tess awoke by habit at a quarter to six. And thank heaven for the habit, she thought, because her alarm clock was still in the living room by the sofa, where she hadn't slept last night.

Slowly, carefully, she eased herself out of Noah's embrace. He muttered in his sleep and reached for her, hauling her back.

Just a minute. Just one more minute, she promised herself, snuggling once more into his arms.

She lay there, counting the seconds, sixty of them, as slowly as she dared, all the while memorizing the feel of the hard warmth of his body next to hers, the muscled weight of his arm wrapped around her, the soft whistle of his breath against her cheek. When she reached fifty, she turned her head and touched her lips to his, left them there, let them savor... *Fifty-seven, fifty-eight, fifty-nine.* Her hand slid up against the back of his neck, cupped it, drew him in. *Sixty.*

The night was over. The loving was over. The dream was over.

Tess sighed and slipped out of bed.

Eight

———

When he woke up, Tess wasn't there.

Noah reached for her instinctively, but the space where she had spent the last hours of the night curled next to him was already cold. Bright winter sun pouring through the window made him realize how late it was. Clearly she had already left for work, and he'd slept far too long.

Still he didn't get up immediately. He couldn't help lying there just a few minutes longer, luxuriating in the memory of Tess in his arms. Loving her was every bit as wonderful as he remembered. Her warmth, her eager responsiveness—everything about her made him lie there and smile.

He heard a rattling sound in the kitchen. Susannah, no doubt. Fixing him breakfast in bed again? He wouldn't have been surprised. Still, once was enough. It was his turn to do something special for her. He got up, stretched and grinned at the sore muscles, which were another reminded of the time spent loving Tess the night before.

Whistling, he went to take a shower.

* * *

He took Susannah out for breakfast. Her mouth wasn't nearly as tender as it had been the day before, so she tucked right into a plate of blueberry pancakes, grinning up at him between bites of pancake and swallows of milk. Noah downed an order of pancakes, two eggs, ham, toast, hash browns and coffee. It was more than he'd eaten in weeks. He felt better than he'd felt since the semi had slapped his van.

He was still whistling when they left the café.

He and Susannah finished the rest of her Christmas shopping before noon. They went home and wrapped the presents and put them under the tree. Then she went over to Janna's to take Libby the gift she'd bought for her that morning.

"Could she maybe stay with you for a while?" Noah asked Janna. "I've got a little more shopping to do."

Janna smiled. "Take your time."

It wouldn't take him long, Noah thought. But before he left, he had some phone calls to make. The first was to the doctor, who told him it was all right if he missed one therapy session. The second was to Taggart.

"Hey, buddy, how you doin'?" Taggart sounded just like his old self.

"Good." Noah leaned back against the sofa and stretched his feet out in front of him, crossing them at the ankles, looking at the photo of Tess and Susannah on the mantel. "I'm doin' good. Great, in fact."

"Ah." He could hear the smile in Taggart's voice. "Reckon you must've talk Tessie around then."

"Well, uh, sort of."

"Sort of? Doesn't sound like you."

"She had a . . . surprise for me."

"What sort of surprise?" Taggart asked cautiously.

Noah hesitated, then told his friend flat out, "We have a daughter."

He explained about Susannah, his words alternately hearty and halting, depending on whether he was talking about the beautiful child he was proud to call his own, or the two weeks that had led up to her conception.

Taggart listened without interrupting. When Noah finished at last, his friend only had two words to say. "Now what?"

"Now I'm gonna marry her, of course," Noah said. There wasn't any doubt in his mind.

It was a little more difficult to tell Tanner, whom he called next.

"Where the hell have you been?" Tanner demanded when he heard Noah's voice. "I've been calling your motel for three days. They said you'd checked out."

"I did."

"You did?" There was a low whistle. "You mean she really took you in? Son of a gun, I don't know how you do it," Tanner said after a moment. "Must be somethin' to have all that sex appeal."

Noah felt curiously nettled. "It isn't just sex appeal."

"Pardon me," Tanner said, amused. "Didn't mean to slight your intellectual allure."

"Maggie been teaching you new words?" Noah grumbled.

"Among other things," Tanner said with a certain amount of smugness. "Haven't you, babe?" he said, and Noah heard him give someone, presumably his long-suffering wife, a smacking kiss.

"Robert! Behave yourself!" Maggie said. But she was laughing and so was he, and Noah smiled, because in a few hours he knew he would be playing those kinds of games with Tess again. But first he had to fill the family in on the new additions. And now that the moment had come to do so, he couldn't find the words.

"What's her last name?" Tanner asked.

"Montgomery."

"And she's a nurse?"

"Uh-huh."

"Met her before, did you?"

"Yeah." Maybe if Tanner kept asking him questions, he'd find the words. How long would it take for his brother to ask, "Father any children with her?"

"Listen, Robert." Noah spoke his brother's name with a twist that was half-fond, half-wry. "Could I maybe talk to your wife?"

"Why?"

"Just let me talk to her."

"You shouldn't be asking what to get me for Christmas at this late date," Tanner teased. Then he sighed and there was another smacking kiss sound. A second later, Maggie's breathless voice said, "Noah, are you all right?"

"Fine. Really," he added, when the one word didn't sound very convincing. "Never been better, in fact."

"Truly? We were so worried. I'd have come with Robert when he came to visit you," Maggie assured him, "but the weather was pretty iffy right then and he didn't want to bring all the boys if there was a chance we might stall somewhere. We'll come as soon as Christmas is over, I promise. Maybe Luke and Jill can come, too. Will that be all right?"

"It'd be fine, Maggie, but I was wonderin' if maybe I could come and see you."

"But I thought the doctor said—"

"I've got to come back," he said quickly. "But he said I could miss one session. We could leave here Christmas afternoon, spend the day after with you, then head back. What do you say?"

Maggie said, "We?"

Noah had always suspected his sister-in-law was pretty sharp.

"That'd be the girl I was tellin' you about," he heard Tanner tell his wife, apparently explaining the "we" on his behalf.

"Her name's Tess," Noah said, bowing to the inevitable.

"Oh, marvelous! And you're bringing her for Christmas? Even better." He could imagine her rubbing her hands together.

"That's not all he's bringing, I hope," Tanner said in the background. "Ask him what he's bringing me now that he's the cham-peen bronc rider in the world."

"Tell him," Noah said to Maggie, "that I'm bringing him a niece."

There was stunned silence on the other end of the line. It was the first time Noah ever remembered his sister-in-law being at a loss for words. "Noah?" she said after a long pause.

"Didn't hang up on you, did he?" Tanner asked.

Maggie didn't answer him. "Noah?" she said again. "Are you serious?"

"Her name's Susannah," he told her. "She's seven. She's beautiful, Mag. The most beautiful little girl in the whole damn world. You wouldn't believe . . ."

"Oh, Noah!" Her tone held a mixture of astonishment, love, pride and concern all at once.

"What's the matter with Noah?" Tanner wanted to know.

"Somethin' wrong with Noah?" he heard Luke ask.

"Tell 'em, Mag, will you?" Noah urged. "I . . . can't."

"But—"

"Please. I'll bring her. And Tess. We'll see you Christmas night."

"I—"

"You're a jewel, Mag. Thanks." And he hung up.

A man who rode bucking broncs for a living couldn't be deemed a complete coward. But brave as he might be on the back of a horse, Noah didn't have the guts to tell Tanner about Susannah.

Maybe it was because of his brother's hasty, but determinedly responsible, first marriage on account of Clare's pregnancy, a far cry from his own less-than-chivalrous treatment of Tess. Maybe it was because his brother's son had died, while he, through no virtue of his own, was now unjustly rewarded with a lively, lovely daughter.

Whatever it was—guilt, immaturity, embarrassment, cowardice, all of the above—Noah couldn't face Tanner, even over the telephone. So he passed the buck to Maggie. She could do it with far more finesse than he could. And he'd be able to face his brothers better when they already knew.

"You haven't gone!" Susannah opened the back door and stared at him.

"Uh, no. Not yet." Noah jerked back to the present. "I was just...makin' a couple of calls first." He shoved away from the counter where he'd been standing. "What are you doing back?"

Susannah flushed. "I was just, uh, getting a game to play with Libby and Jeff." She started past him when the phone rang.

She picked it up. "Hello?" There was a pause. "This is Susannah," she said, and Noah noticed how careful she was not to turn the *s*'s into *th*'s. He smiled.

Her eyes widened. "My uncle Robert?" She shot Noah a glance, then ran her tongue over her lips.

"What?" Noah straightened sharply. *That was Tanner on the phone?* He almost snatched the receiver out of her hand. Only a shred of common courtesy stopped him. That and the slow smile that he could see spreading over Susannah's face.

"I'm seven," she was saying now, apparently in response to one of Tanner's questions. "And a half." There was a pause. "April 12th."

Tanner must have asked when her birthday was. Noah's fingers itched to take the phone. Susannah was still smiling as she listened to whatever Tanner was saying.

"I know. My dad told me about them. We got presents for them." Tanner's boys, obviously. Susannah giggled. "I don't know if my mom will let me baby-sit yet."

Noah goggled at the thought.

"'Kay," Susannah was saying. "I'll see you tomorrow, Uncle Robert."

Noah expected her to hang up.

She said, "Hi, Uncle Luke."

So then he had to stand and tap his toes and shift from one foot to the other and wonder what Luke was saying to her. Whatever it was, it made her giggle and glance at him and then giggle again.

"Oh, no, he's really brave," she said at last, giving him another look. "You should see him when he goes to therapy. It hurts a lot, but he works really hard."

So Noah supposed that all his effort yesterday hadn't been totally in vain. He smiled at his daughter.

"He said I was brave, too," Susannah told Luke. "'Cause yesterday when he was baby-sitting me, I ran into a tree an' knocked out my tooth an' I didn't even cry...much." She paused. "No, he was careful," she said. "It was my fault."

Noah scowled.

Susannah grinned at him. "Do you want to talk to him?" she asked Luke. "Oh, okay. Yeah, I can hardly wait to meet you, too. Bye."

She hung up and looked at Noah, starry-eyed. "That was my uncle Robert and my uncle Luke," she told him. "They said we're gonna see them tomorrow."

He nodded, pleased now that Tanner had called, though a few minutes ago he'd done his share of worrying. He should have known his brothers would welcome a niece with open arms. They'd welcome Tess, too. And as far as what they might say to him privately, well, it was nothing he didn't deserve.

"I thought maybe we could drive up there tomorrow— after Santa comes," he added, in case Susannah was worried.

She didn't seem to be. "That'll be neat. An' then I'll get to see my cousins." She said the word with relish and grinned up at him again. "I always wanted a sister or brother," she confided. "But I don't care so much if I've got cousins."

It was on the tip of his tongue to tell her that perhaps he and Tess would see what they could do about a brother or sister for her, too. But he thought it was something he'd better talk over with Tess first.

"I'm sure they'll be glad to have you, too," he said.

They were sitting side by side on the couch, their dark heads bent over a book that Susannah held across her knees, when Tess walked in the door. They looked up at her with identical smiles that made her heart turn over in her chest.

"Look, Mom! Noah's showin' me his scrapbook."

A scrapbook of his rodeo days, Tess presumed. The chronicle of his travels down the road, culminating in the gold-buckle finals just over two weeks ago.

"Come see," Susannah commanded.

Noah flushed. "You don't have—"

But Tess slipped off her boots and hung up her coat, then said, "Let me see." It would be salutary, she told herself. It would remind her, in case she let her heart get in the way of her common sense, what really mattered to Noah Tanner. His scrapbook would point out very clearly who he really was.

So she got a considerable shock when she peered over Susannah's shoulder and found that she was looking at a childish drawing of a fat man in a red suit and a bunch of stick animals she supposed must be reindeer.

"Noah drew that," Susannah said, "when he was three."

"I wasn't much of an artist," he muttered. "Come on, Suse. We don't have to bore your mother with a bunch of old scribblings."

"I'm not bored," Tess said. Indeed, she was enthralled. "What is this?"

"It's Noah's scrapbook. I was tellin' you," Susannah said impatiently. "He made it with his mother when he was a little boy."

"We all did." Noah sounded almost defensive. The color in his cheeks was still high. "Me and Tan—I mean, Robert—and Luke. We put Christmas cards we liked in 'em, and drawings and letters to Santa. They were mostly Christmas books. But my mother put some snapshots in, too. After my dad died, we had to move, and my brother was, well, hurt, I guess. And angry. He was throwing everything out, and—" he shrugged "—the scrapbooks were about all that was left of when my mother was alive. So I saved 'em."

The scrapbook Susannah held was rather shabby look-ing and water spotted, Tess noted now. There were two others on the coffee table, both equally worn.

"I had 'em stored at a friend's in Durango," Noah ex-plained. "I'd pretty much forgot about them until last Christmas, when I was at Tanner and Maggie's. An' damned if Tanner wasn't helping Jared make a scrapbook. He shrugged kinda awkward and said, 'I was thinkin' about the ones we made.' An' then he said, 'You were so young, you probably don't even remember.'" Noah grinned remi-niscently. "I didn't tell him I had them. I thought I'd give him his this Christmas. I picked 'em up on my way to Ve-gas for the finals, because I knew I was goin' to his place right after. I just remembered this afternoon that they were still in the van."

"We went to the mechanic place—"

"Body shop," Noah explained.

"—And got 'em," Susannah finished. "Come look," she invited again, and inched over so she was practically sitting in Noah's lap.

And Tess, in spite of her better judgment, was captivated by the chance to know the child Noah had been. She sat down.

He'd wanted to impress her. He'd wanted her to come home, take one look at him and remember the virile, eager man who'd made love to her the night before.

Instead she was seeing him as a three-year-old. Worse, a one-year-old.

It was bad enough having your daughter see a picture of you with your Christmas stocking and your diaper half falling down. It was downright mortifying to have the woman you'd made love to for hours take one look at the one-year-old Noah Tanner, smile, swallow a laugh and say, "What cute cheeks."

Noah didn't think he'd ever been so embarrassed in his life. He started to shut the scrapbook, but Tess and Susannah pulled it away from him. Then they sat there smiling and simpering at what a cute little boy he'd been, and what a jolly little snowman he'd drawn, and how handsome he and his big brothers had looked sitting in a row on the old runner sled in front of the house.

Finally, thank heavens, Susannah had seen enough. She wiggled and then bounced off the sofa and went to let the cat out. But even when Noah said, "You've seen all there is to see, believe me," Tess wasn't ready to relinquish the book.

"I thought Suse looked like me," she said wonderingly. "Except for the eyes, of course. They were always yours. But see how much she looks like Robert?"

"That's 'cause he was seven in that picture," Noah said. "Same as her." It was the last one in the book, the one with the three of them on the sled. It was the last Christmas his mother had been alive.

Tess shook her head. "It's not just the age. See? She has his jaw."

"Stubborn," Noah said. "Righteous. Determined."

Tess laughed. "How did you know?"

"I know Tanner."

"You told me he was the nice one of you three," she reminded him.

"He is." Noah reflected on the phone call Tanner had made. He'd probably been calling back to chew him out for not telling him about Susannah himself. But when she'd answered the phone, he'd completely charmed her instead.

"I think they're both nice," Susannah said as she came back into the room.

Tess frowned. "How do you know?"

"I talked to 'em on the phone. We're going there tomorrow."

Tess turned her frown in his direction.

"I just called them today to—to tell them about...you. Both of you," Noah said quickly. "And one thing led to another and, well, I know you've got Christmas and the day after off, and the doc said I can miss therapy once, so I thought it would be a good way to get the family together—"

"And I can see my cousins!" Susannah exclaimed.

"Are you sure—"

"Absolutely," Noah said. His gaze met hers. "They want you to come. *I* want you to come." His gaze beseeched her. He would have preferred to bring it up after everything was settled tonight. He should have realized that Susannah would take matters into her own hands.

Tess hesitated, then nodded slowly. It wasn't the enthusiastic response Noah had hoped for. But then he hadn't asked her the all-important question yet. And she obviously had no idea he was going to.

He swallowed a smile and allowed Tess her reluctance—for now.

It wasn't easy keeping a secret.

Right before dinner, when Noah was sitting on the living room rug with Susannah, helping her build a manger with Lincoln Logs, he'd glanced up to see Tess standing in the doorway to the kitchen, looking at them wistfully. He'd wanted to get up and go to her then. The ring was burning a hold in his pocket. But he wanted the time to be right. He wanted it to be just the two of them.

Then the phone rang and she went to answer it.

"It's for you," she called from the kitchen.

Tanner again? Noah wondered. Or Luke?

Tess didn't say. She barely looked at him when he came in to pick up the phone.

"Hey, Noah, is she as pretty as she sounds?" It was a rodeo buddy named Jim Jackson, a guy he and Taggart had traveled with on and off during the past year.

Noah grinned. "Prettier, if you want to know the truth."

"You always did land on your feet. Taggart told me where you were," Jim said. "Heard you almost bought the farm couple weeks back, you 'n' Taggart both. Tough luck. How ya doin' now?"

"Better," Noah said. He was watching Tess move around the kitchen, enjoying the sight of the inch or so of midriff he was able to glimpse when she stretched to get a bowl from the top shelf of the cupboard. "Much better."

"Reckon so, with a pretty lady to kiss it and make it well. Glad to hear it. So, when you gonna be ready to go?"

"Go?" Noah echoed. Hell, he hadn't even thought about that.

"Figured to head on down to Odessa for New Year's," Jim told him. "Good money down there. Might as well start off the year right. You game?"

"Not for Odessa. Not by a long shot. I'm stuck in Laramie for the time being, trying to get my knee back in shape." He told Jim about the thrice-weekly therapy sessions.

Jim whistled. "You gonna be up for Denver?"

"Don't know." He hadn't thought that far ahead.

"Don't know much, do you?" Jim was grinning; Noah could tell.

"No, but I'm learning," he said, still watching Tess move. God, she was lovely, even when she was setting the table and pretending to ignore him. Except he didn't want to be ignored. "Gotta go," he said. "You have a good Christmas." He hung up, stepped behind Tess, who stood at the counter dishing up potatoes, and dropped a kiss on the back of her neck.

She jumped. "Stop that!" She shot a worried glance toward the living room.

He scowled. "Hey, it was just a kiss. First chance I've had to do it today. You were gone when I woke up."

Tess's cheeks grew red. She rubbed the back of her neck and muttered something under her breath. Then she said, "Get washed up, both of you. It's time for dinner."

Susannah must have heard, because she appeared in the doorway. "I'm starving. Are you starving?" she asked Noah.

He looked at Tess, devouring her with his eyes. "You bet I am."

She blushed throughout the entire meal. She also avoided his gaze. Was she thinking about what they were going to do when the lights went off tonight? Was she as eager as he was? He hoped so.

"Stop wiggling in your chair, Susannah," Tess said sharply. "Christmas won't get here any faster if you do."

Susannah stuck out her lower lip and poked at the potatoes on her plate. "It takes forever," she complained. "It takes days and days, an' when it's finally Christmas Eve, it seems like the hours take days and days, too."

Noah, reaching into his pocket and touching the small velvet box with the ring he'd bought in it, knew exactly what she meant.

"When do we leave for church?" Susannah asked.

Tess glanced at her watch. "Forty-five minutes. Enough time for you to eat a good dinner and then help me with the dishes."

"You're coming, aren't you?" Susannah asked Noah. "I'm singing in the children's choir, then Mom's singing in the real one."

"I wouldn't miss it for the world."

They got to the church well before the candlelight service was to begin. It was the same small brick building Tess had brought him to eight years before. Then, they had come on a Sunday morning, on a day filled with bright summer sunlight. Tonight the sky was dark, with low, gray clouds, and all the color came from within. The stained-glass windows shone in jewel-like splendor as they headed up the walk toward the heavy double doors.

It had started to snow again, and for once the wind had stopped, so the flakes floated gently down, dusting the sidewalk and their jackets and coming to rest in lacy profusion on Susannah's dark hair. She was walking between them, holding Tess's hand in her right and Noah's in her left. Like a family, Noah thought, looking down and smiling at her. Susannah tipped her head back and caught snowflakes on her tongue.

He saw Tess give her a fleeting look of disapproval. But then she shrugged and smiled. "I can't say anything. I've done it myself," she admitted.

"When you were a kid?" Noah asked.

"Yes." She grinned. "And this morning."

He laughed out loud, and Susannah looked up at them both, surprised, and squeezed his hand harder.

As soon as they got inside the door, she shed her jacket and handed it to her mother, then darted toward the choir loft. All at once she stopped and turned back. "Where are you going to be sitting?" she asked Noah.

He looked at Tess for instructions. She hesitated, then pointed to one of the side pews toward the back of the church. "You can meet him here," she said.

When Susannah had vanished up the steps, she explained, "The children's choir will do the caroling before the service. Then they'll come down and the adult choir will sing. There's a place in the front for the kids who come without their families or whose parents are in the choir. Usually she sits there. But since you're here..." Her voice trailed off. She looked a little wary, a little worried.

"Oh, here you are, Tess!" A jovial older lady appeared at Tess's side. "We're just going over the offertory down the hall. Can you come?"

"Go ahead," Noah said. "I'll be right there."

Tess looked as if she might have wanted to say something else, then shrugged.

"We'll be waiting for you." He dropped a kiss on the end of her nose and saw the choir lady's eyes widen. Tess blushed, then turned and hustled her away.

There was something infinitely soothing and absolutely right about sitting in a pew in a candle-lit church on Christmas Eve and listening to the clear, high voices of the children's choir sing carols he remembered singing himself long ago. Last year he'd gone with Tanner and Maggie and Jared to the little country church closest to the ranch. Maggie had been enormously pregnant, and Tanner had been sweating about whether or not they would make it through the service before she gave birth. Noah had hassled him afterward about being such a worrywart.

"Yeah, well, you have a kid next Christmas and let's see how you do," Tanner had retorted.

Noah smiled. Little had they known, either of them...

The last of the carols died away. There was a bumping and thumping overhead, and then the sound of giggles and whispers as thirty or so pairs of feet clattered down the bare wooden stairs. Seconds later Susannah climbed over two couples sitting in the same pew and wedged herself next to Noah.

He slid his arm around her and she looked up at him. "How'd we do?"

"You were wonderful."

It was nothing but the truth. She was the most wonderful child he'd ever known. His nephews were pretty great, but there was no one on earth, in Noah's opinion, who could compare with this little girl.

She squeezed his hand for just a second, then pulled away and slipped down onto the kneeler, bending her head, closing her eyes and folding her hands. He watched while her lips moved in silent prayer.

Then she sat back again next to him. "I was saying thank you," she told him, "for you."

Noah spent a good part of the service saying thank you, too.

You never had to put together horses.

It was one of the advantages of giving a pony for Christmas. There was no sprocket A to be connected to flange B. No dohickey G to be attached to thingamajig H. And no chain that slipped and slid no matter what you did.

Noah had disappeared into the basement as soon as they got home, so Tess got the job of urging Susannah off to bed. For once she didn't get any argument.

"The sooner I go to sleep, the sooner it's morning," Susannah had said as she'd climbed the stairs. "I know. I know." Then she'd glanced back over her mother's shoulder, and her gaze lit on Noah. "Maybe I won't get anything else," she said. "Since I got what I wanted." But she didn't look too worried, and Tess just shook her head.

"Up the steps with you, young lady."

"I'm going," Susannah grumbled, then once more she turned back. "Will you come and kiss me goodnight?" she had called to Noah.

"I will."

But in the meantime, he had to get started on the bike.

It would have been easier if he'd been able to get one already built—or even mostly assembled. But by Christmas Eve, as the sales clerk explained, all those had long since been sold. What Noah had was in a box, and when he spread it out on the basement floor, the only things immediately identifiable were the wheels, the handlebars, the chain and the pedals. It was going to be a long night.

Tess appeared at the top of the stairs. "What are you..." She stopped and stared. "Oh, Noah. You shouldn't—"

He looked up from where he was squatting. "Don't tell me I shouldn't have. That's pretty apparent," he said wryly. "I hope you're mechanical, 'cause I'm sure as hell not. I can do a tractor if I have to, and a windmill in a pinch, but I'm a country boy, and this country boy doesn't know a thing about bikes."

Tess shook her head, smiling, and started down the stairs. "Go say good-night to Susannah. She's waiting."

He unfolded from the floor and started toward the steps, meeting her as she reached the bottom. He aimed a kiss at her, but she ducked past so fast he barely hit her ear.

"Go on," she urged him. "You don't want her to come looking for you."

Noah nodded. "I'll be back."

Susannah was tucked snugly into her bed, her hands folded on top of the quilt, when he appeared in the doorway. She smiled and lifted her arms toward him.

He bent down and gave her a hug. She wrapped her arms around his neck tightly, clinging for a long minute, then almost reluctantly she lay back down again. When he straightened, her fingers still clenched around his as she looked at him, her eyes as blue and serious as his own. "I love you."

Noah's throat tightened. He swallowed hard. "I love you, too, sweetheart." He bent and dropped a kiss on her lips, then brushed her hair back from her forehead. "You better go to sleep now or Santa won't come."

Susannah gave him a conspiratorial smile. "He always comes," she said confidently. "Even when I get up really early, he's always been here."

"Is that so? Well," Noah said, thinking of the disassembled bike scattered across the basement floor, "you might want to maybe sleep in and give him a little more time this year. He could be running a bit late."

"I'll try," Susannah promised, shutting her eyes.

Noah reached the door and turned out the light. "Merry Christmas, Suse," he said, glancing back at his daughter in the darkness.

She raised her head. "Good night, Daddy."

Daddy. She'd called him Daddy.

He didn't realize how much he'd wanted to hear it until at last the word had crossed her lips.

He hadn't disputed her calling him "Noah." He hadn't suggested anything else. He knew that fatherhood wasn't something taken lightly; it had to be earned. Not that he figured he'd done much in the way of earning it yet. But she was giving him a chance. If he'd worried at all that she might object to his marrying Tess and becoming a permanent part of their lives, that worry was assuaged. He dipped his hand into the pocket of his jeans and fingered the velvet box.

He was smiling all the way down the basement steps.

Tess put the bike together.

She was well on her way to accomplishing it by the time he got back to the basement, the smile still on his face. He stared at the bike, then at her, in astonishment. "How'd you do that?"

"I read the directions."

"Yeah, but..." He shook his head, dazed.

"Hand me the wrench," Tess said, jerking her chin toward one lying near his foot.

Noah handed it to her. She used it. "Now the other one." He handed it over. She used it, too. She stood the bike up and checked the way the chain moved. It didn't slide; it didn't slip. Noah's brows lifted.

"Impressive," he murmured.

Tess colored. "I hope you don't mind," she said quickly. "I just thought I might help out a little while you were upstairs."

"I don't mind," Noah said in his best magnanimous tone.

"I didn't mean to horn in," she apologized.

"No problem. No problem at all. Anytime you want to put a bike together, I won't stand in your way."

She stood up quickly. "You can finish."

Pretty much all that was left to do was put on the seat and the pedals. He figured he could manage that. "I bought a bottle of brandy when I was out today," he told her. "It's in the bag on the counter. Why don't you go up and pour us each some while I finish down here?"

"Brandy?" she said doubtfully.

"It's Christmas. We're celebrating."

She looked a little wary and a little worried, but she nodded. "All right." Still she shot him an apprehensive look over her shoulder as she went up the stairs.

It took him almost as much time to get the seat on and adjusted and the pedals moving smoothly as it had taken Tess to put together the rest of the bike. But finally he got it done and stood back to contemplate the job. For a rookie Santa, he hadn't done all that badly, although it was a good thing he'd had a Ms. Claus around to help him out. Otherwise he might have been at it all night.

Tess was sitting at the kitchen table with two snifters of brandy ready and waiting when he came up the stairs.

"You bought snifters, too," she said wonderingly. "I've never had brandy before."

He didn't make a habit of drinking it himself. But tonight was special. Besides, he'd never proposed marriage before, either.

He picked up one of the snifters, then reached out and took her by the arm, urging her to her feet. "Come on," he said and drew her with him into the living room.

The only lights came from the glowing fire in the fireplace and the tiny colored bulbs on the Christmas tree. Noah led Tess to the sofa. She sat down, clutching the snifter. He sat next to her, turned and faced her.

Her eyes were wide and luminous, her dark hair curling softly around her face. He wanted to bury his hands in it. He wanted to touch his lips to hers, to take her to the same magical place where they'd spent the night before.

And he would—just as soon as he said, "I have a present for you."

Tess blinked. "Present? Tonight? But I thought we'd open them in the morn—"

"Not this one," Noah said. He fished in his pocket, pulled out the tiny velvet box and opened it. A simply set diamond solitaire winked in the firelight. He picked it out of the box and held it out to Tess.

Her eyes got even wider. Her complexion seemed to pale. She looked at him with an expression he couldn't put a name to. "What is it?" Her voice sounded equal parts hoarse and incredulous.

He smiled. "An engagement ring. The wedding ring is upstairs in the bedroom." He took her hand to slip it on. Her fingers clenched into a fist.

"What's wrong? Don't you like it?"

"It—it's lovely." She seemed almost to choke on the words. She pulled her hand away, twisting her fingers together in her lap.

He snapped the box shut. "Tess? What's the matter with you? I'm asking you to marry me." He reached out and touched her chin, tipping her face up so he could look straight into her eyes.

She stared at him, stricken.

"Don't you want to marry me?"

Her fingers knotted even tighter. She shook her head and looked away. "No."

Nine

It wasn't fair.

How could he ask her to *marry* him? How could he take the one thing she'd wanted more than anything in the world and offer it to her for all the wrong reasons?

"What do you mean, no?"

It seemed like an age had passed since she'd said that one simple, yet monumentally difficult, word. In reality Tess supposed it hadn't been more than a few seconds, thirty at most. She looked up to see Noah gazing at her, his expression a mixture of astonishment and hurt.

Hurt?

No, not really, she assured herself. Not unless it was the sort of hurt that came with having one's charitable proposition turned down.

She drew a slow, careful breath, mustering calm, summoning strength. "I mean, thank you for the offer, but I don't want to marry you."

"Why not?"

Damn it! Couldn't he just leave it alone? What sort of man asked for an explanation when his proposal had been rejected?

"I don't love you."

She could tell from his expression that, of all the reasons she might have offered, that was one he hadn't expected. He looked as if she'd knocked the air right out of him. Something akin to a shudder ran through him. She saw his knuckles whiten as he gripped the velvet box, as if he would crush it in his hand.

"I see," he said.

He didn't—for which she was profoundly grateful.

"Thank you for the offer, of course," she said now, with as much lightness of tone as she could manage. "It's very kind of you, but—"

"*Kind?*" The word seemed to explode from him. "You think I'm offering to be kind?"

Tess gave a tiny, awkward shrug. "Well, I'm sure you have a variety of motives—"

He gaped at her. "You make it sound like I'm some criminal!"

She shook her head. "No." Though if the truth were known, he was murdering her heart. "I just... don't want to marry you—whatever your reasons. It wasn't what we agreed to."

"Agreed?" he echoed hollowly.

Tess stood up. "We agreed that you could stay until after Christmas. And that's it. Now, if you'll excuse me, I want to check on Susannah. If she's asleep, I can bring down the gifts from Santa. Then I want to go to bed. I'm really very tired." She fled up the stairs without waiting for a response.

* * *

She was afraid he'd left.

When she came back carrying gifts, after she'd made sure Susannah was asleep, he wasn't there. She thought he might have gone back down to the basement. She didn't want to look. She *didn't* look until more than an hour had passed, all the gifts had been set beneath the tree and she still hadn't heard a sound from down below. Finally she ventured to the top of the steps and peered down.

"Noah?" She said his name tentatively.

When she got no reply, she dared to creep down the steps. The bike was sitting there, ready to be put under the tree. Of Noah there was no sign. Tess looked all around the basement. She looked all around the house. Then she opened the front door.

There were recent footprints in the snow-covered steps. They led down the walk, out the gate and beyond.

He was gone.

And what was she supposed to tell Susannah in the morning? Not the truth, surely. Susannah, whose fondest unspoken wish had to be that her parents would get together, would never understand why Tess had said no.

"Damn you, Noah!" she raged in a ragged whisper. Noah-the-cat came to peer out the door from between her feet. He poked his nose out far enough to get snowflakes on his whiskers. Noah-the-cat came back in.

Tess watched him walk across to the hearth and turn around, then settle in on the rug. He yawned. He purred.

She started to cry.

She didn't even realize it at first. It was only when she felt something sliding down her cheek that she realized the unexpected wetness was tears. She swiped at them, irritated. She didn't want to cry. She'd shed enough tears over Noah Tanner years ago. She was past that, damn it. Past him!

But the tears wouldn't stop coming.

It was a quarter past two and she was huddled in a ball on the sofa bed when she heard the front door open, and a snow-dusted, dark shape came in. Tess couldn't help it; she breathed a sigh of relief. Not that he was safe—that went without question. Rather, that he was back, and now she wouldn't have to think of some lie to tell Susannah.

In the dim glow from the streetlight outside, she watched as he hung his jacket in the closet by the front door. She saw him lean against the wall and tug off his boots, then set them silently next to her shoes and Susannah's smaller ones. He stood there for a moment, looking down at them.

Then he gave his head a shake, scattering the snowflakes that had frosted his dark hair, and limped into the room.

Tess shut her eyes. The footsteps came closer, then stopped. She could feel him standing over her, staring down at her in the darkness. She didn't move, didn't breathe.

Finally she heard him sigh. The limping footsteps moved on.

If Susannah noticed that her mother seemed more tired than usual on Christmas morning, she didn't remark on it. If she noted that Noah's smiles didn't quite reach his eyes, she never said a word. She was thrilled with her bike, wanting to take it out in the nine inches of new snow and ride it.

"I can wear my new sweater and my new jacket," she told her mother.

"And shovel the walk with your new snow shovel so you can ride it," Noah said, which was the most lighthearted thing he'd managed to say all morning long.

"I didn't get a snow shovel, Daddy," Susannah retorted, giggling.

So he was still *Daddy* this morning, even if the word did make Tess's already ivory complexion pale even more. Noah watched her reaction as she sat curled on the sofa amid the crumpled wrapping paper, sipping tea and holding the cat in her lap. She looked ill.

No worse than he felt.

Damn it, he still couldn't believe she'd said no!

It didn't make sense. Anyone could see it would be the best thing for everyone if they got married. Susannah would have both her parents. Tess wouldn't have to do everything alone anymore. And he would have the family he wanted, the family he'd begun to think he'd never have. And that didn't even take into account how good he and Tess were in bed together!

He didn't suppose she'd want him bringing that up.

She apparently didn't want him bringing up anything about last night, either. The only mention she made of it was just as Susannah came down to see what Santa had brought. Tess had still been on the sofa with the comforter tucked around her when Susannah had tugged Noah down the stairs. Her eyes had been like saucers when she'd caught sight of the bike. She'd looked from it to both her parents in mute astonishment.

"I never thought—!" she said at last. And then she was jabbering a mile a minute, talking about how wonderful it was.

She never heard Tess say to Noah in a low voice, "Thank you for coming back. It would have been hard to explain to her."

"Try explaining it to me sometime," he'd said harshly.

But she'd just shaken her head. "No."

And after that, she hadn't said another word. Now the gifts had been opened, the bike ridden in small circles in the living room, the new sweater and jacket tried on, the various and sundry other gifts they'd given each other exclaimed over. A breakfast of freshly baked cinnamon rolls and fruit cups had been eaten.

Susannah finished the last roll and wiped her mouth on her napkin. "When do we go to Uncle Robert's?"

Tess and Noah looked at each other. Then Tess looked away. "I don't know," she began, "if it's such a good idea—"

"They're expecting us," Noah cut in before she could worm her way out of it. Maybe it would be awkward; maybe he'd be sorry. Hell, he was already sorry. It couldn't get much worse. But Susannah had a right to get to know her uncles and aunts and cousins.

He saw Tess hesitate, saw Susannah, aware suddenly that something wasn't quite right, look at her mother beseechingly. Tess looked from her daughter to Noah and back again. Finally she sighed and shrugged. "Fine. We'll go."

"Uncle Robert says they've got horses," Susannah told her mother, as if she was an adult promising a child a treat. "You'll like that."

Tess gave her a reluctant smile. "Yes, I expect I will."

She obviously didn't expect to like much else. But she swallowed whatever other objections might have occurred to her and helped Susannah and Noah load the car.

"When're we gonna get there?" Susannah asked, bouncing on the back seat before they were barely out of Laramie.

"Don't start," Tess said.

It was a long drive, over six hours from door to door. Happily, Susannah was exhausted enough from the excitement of the holiday that she slept for a good part of the trip. Tess and Noah took turns sharing the driving. Tess did most of it because Noah's leg still bothered him. Not that he talked about it.

They drove the entire afternoon and, once Susannah was asleep, neither one of them said a word.

* * *

Susannah was in heaven. She had uncles who doted on her, aunts who chatted and laughed with her and little cousins who thought she was the best playmate in the world. She had a pony to ride, the grandson of the hired man to show her all the best hideouts in the barn and five eight-week-old golden-retriever puppies to entertain her.

Whether Noah and Tess were in hell or simply in purgatory depended on what was happening at any particular moment. Noah, seeing ever more clearly the happiness of his formerly lone wolf brothers as they hugged and teased their wives, ached at the thought of never having that kind of closeness with Tess and Susannah. Tess, seeing women she liked instinctively happily married to men so like Noah that she could scarcely believe it, was pierced by sadness that that joy would never be hers. Noah, watching Tanner roughhouse gently with his three sons until he felt Susannah's arms go around his waist and pull him into a rough-housing match of their own, hated knowing just how few chances he would have to show this little girl how much she meant to him. Tess, watching the quiet contentment and easy authority with which Tanner handled his brood, and the gentle awe with which Luke still treated his firstborn son, ached at the knowledge that Susannah would never experience such day-to-day joy with her father.

The old family albums Noah gave his brothers brought tears to their eyes.

"I thought they were lost years ago," Tanner said, shaking his head in disbelief. "Look, Mag!" He called his wife to come sit beside him and leaf through the pages. "This is the horse I was tellin' you about. And here's that old sled I wiped out on."

"Let's see," Maggie said eagerly.

And as she tucked herself in next to him, Tess felt a pang of envy at their closeness, at the past and the future they would share.

"My, you were a handsome devil even when you were five," she heard Jill tell Luke moments later.

"Me?" Luke flushed and ducked his head. Tess was amazed. She'd never imagined a fast-lane Hollywood stunt coordinator like Luke Tanner would have a bashful bone in his body. Apparently, where his wife's compliments were concerned, he did. She felt a little self-conscious overhearing, as if she was eavesdropping.

"They're still lovebirds," growled Everett Warren, the old cowboy who was Tanner's right-hand man.

"It's nice," Tess said, and tried to keep the envy out of voice.

She had expected to feel awkward, to be treated coolly or at least sceptically by Tanner and Luke and their wives. She was welcomed with open arms.

"We were so worried when we thought Noah was going to be alone for the holidays," Maggie confided later.

They were sitting in the living room after a sumptuous dinner, she and Tess on the sofa, Jill, who was nursing baby Keith, in the rocker by the fireplace. Tess could hear Susannah and Jared giggling and talking upstairs. The twins, Nick and Seth, as alike as two peas with their dark hair and deep blue eyes and the promise of heart-stopping Tanner grins, were already sound asleep in their cribs.

The other Tanner brothers were in the kitchen doing dishes.

Tess had been amazed, but the other women seemed to take it as a matter of course when, after everyone helped clear the table, their husbands shooed them out of the kitchen.

"It's a tradition," Maggie explained. "The first year we were together, Robert said I did so much cooking and baking for the holidays that, just once, he wanted me to sit down and put my feet up. So that night he and Luke and Noah did the dishes. And then the next year I was nursing Jared when it came time to do the dishes—" she grinned "—not even on purpose. And so they did them again. And after, well, Robert said it was good for them, too. They rarely talk to each other. Christmas night they talk. And," she said cheerfully, "we can talk to you."

Tess gulped.

Jill smiled at her. "We don't do the third degree, so don't worry. We're just glad to all be together. And glad you're here, too."

"So am I," Tess said, and found it was the truth.

"A new tradition," Maggie said. "Every year we add a bride."

Tess bit her lip and looked away.

"Oh, heavens. I'm sorry," Maggie said quickly. "Me and my big mouth. And here I am, jumping the gun as usual. Robert says I take too much for granted. But if Noah doesn't come through and—"

"He has," Tess said softly, before Maggie could finish the warning. "I said no."

Both women looked at her, their eyes wide in the room's sudden silence. Upstairs, the childish laughter continued. The low sound of Noah and his brothers' voices coming from the kitchen rubbed against Tess's battered emotions. She pressed her lips together and shook her head mutely.

"You can't tell me you don't love him," Maggie said quietly after a moment.

Tess didn't dare try to tell her that. She might have been able to convince Noah, but she'd seen enough of his sisters-in-law in the few hours she'd been here to be sure she couldn't lie anywhere near well enough to convince them that she didn't love him.

"So what's the problem?" Jill asked, her expression serious, gentle, yet concerned when Tess didn't reply.

Tess shook her head again. "It wouldn't work," she said finally, when it became clear that they weren't going to take silence for an answer.

"You don't trust him?" Maggie said.

"Has he ever lied to you?" asked Jill.

"Maybe he has," Maggie reflected softly, staring into the fire. "Robert did a lot of lying—to me and to himself."

Jill smiled. "So did Luke, come to that."

They both looked at Tess sympathetically.

There was a sudden crash and a howl from upstairs.

"Uh-oh," Maggie said, jumping up to go see what had happened. "I knew it was too good to last."

"I like her," Luke said. He picked up a glass from the drainer and began to dry it.

"Me, too," Tanner said as he put away the ones Luke had already dried.

"She's the best little girl in the world," Noah agreed readily, his hands deep in soapy water.

"Not Susannah," Luke said. "We all know that goes without saying. I'm talking about Tess."

"Me, too," said Tanner.

Which Noah had suspected all along. But a little determined misunderstanding seemed like the better part of common sense. He'd hoped it would deflect their questions.

"When're you gonna marry her?" Tanner asked.

So much for the usefulness of being deliberately obtuse. Noah reached for another dirty plate and dunked it in the soapy water. "I'm not."

Both his brothers stopped dead and stared at him.

"The hell you say!" Tanner practically jumped down his throat.

"What the—!" Luke almost leapt right after him. Then he stopped and took a close look at his younger brother's face. "What happened? What's wrong?"

Both of them closed in on him then. Noah avoided their eyes, shaking his head, staring down at the water in the sink. "Nothin'," he mumbled.

Neither of his brothers spoke for a moment. They looked at each other. "Hang in there," Tanner finally said.

"Don't quit," Luke advised. A grin quirked the corner of his mouth for just a moment. "Remember? You told me, cowboys don't."

"Surprised you didn't hit me in the mouth," Noah muttered. God, he'd been an overbearing son-of-a-gun in those days. "Should've."

His brothers looked at each other again, then at him.

"If you come back without her in the spring," Tanner said, "maybe we will."

If threats would have got Tess to agree to marry him, Noah might have tried some. If pleading or cajoling would have worked, he'd have given that some thought, too. But if she didn't love him, what more was there to say? What good would it do?

And if, come spring, Tanner and Luke gave it to him on the chin, well, it was no more than he deserved. The thing was, Noah figured he'd deserved it more eight years ago. Back then he might have been able to do something about marrying Tess. Back then she had loved him.

But he'd had other goals, other dreams.

He'd loved her, too—at least as much as he'd been capable of loving anyone in those days. But more than a relationship, more than a marriage, he'd wanted to be the bronc-riding champion of the world.

And now he was.

He was proud of his gold buckle; he couldn't deny that. He was proud of his perseverance, his determination, his skill—all the things that had gone into making him number one.

But hearing everyone call him "Champ" for the year, as nice as it might be, was somehow far less appealing than hearing one little girl call him "Daddy" every day for the rest of his life.

But Tess didn't love him.

He didn't know if Susannah was simply exhausted from the excitement of the visit to Tanner and Maggie's or if she somehow sensed the mood of her parents as they headed back to Laramie the following afternoon. Whatever it was, the eager babble they'd listened to on the way up and the joyful noise they'd heard all the time she was with her cousins gave way to pensiveness when their time on the ranch had run out and they headed south once more.

Several times Noah thought she must be sleeping. But when he glanced over his shoulder, it was to find her staring out the window, a look of deep thoughtfulness on her face.

Tess wasn't talking much, either. She did sleep some, or at least pretended to. He hoped that, in her sleep, she would slip his way and rest her head against his arm, so that he could slide it around her and draw her close and feel the softness of her curls against his fingers as he drove. But she leaned toward the door, her head resting on the window, the cold glass obviously preferable to the warmth of his arm.

When it was her turn to drive, Noah debated doing a little sleeping and perhaps a little drifting himself. But though years of going down the road had taught him to sleep in a car at the drop of a hat, they'd also taught him that resting his head on Taggart Jones's shoulder wasn't the way to go. And the habit of leaning against the door was so deeply ingrained that he couldn't even fake sagging the other way. So he sat upright and silent all the way home.

Susannah was still asleep when Tess pulled into the driveway.

"I'll carry her in," Noah said.

"I can wake her up."

"No." He wanted to carry her, and he didn't give Tess a chance to argue. He got out and pulled the seat forward, then reached into the back to scoop his daughter up into his arms. It was an awkward angle. The movement hurt his still-somewhat-tender ribs, and the lifting put pressure on his knee that he was sure the doctor would frown on.

He didn't care. He wanted to hold Susannah in his arms. God only knew how many more times he'd be able to do it. He could stretch out his time with them for a few days longer. Maybe, if Tess allowed it, until the first of the year. But then their agreement would really have been pushed to the limit. His leg would be well enough—or it wouldn't, and he'd need surgery. But in any case, he'd be gone.

He hugged Susannah's slender form against his chest as he carried her into the house and up the stairs to her bedroom.

Tess followed, carrying her small duffel bag and two model horses that Susannah's cousins had given her for Christmas. "I'll get her into pajamas."

Noah settled the sleeping child on the bed and straightened. "Then I'll unload the car." Just like an old married couple, he thought as he went back outside.

An old married couple with no future. He found it hard to swallow past the lump in his throat.

He carried in the rest of their gear and then the presents Tanner and Maggie and Luke and Jill had given them. In the last package was a small stack of photos that Jill had taken with an instant camera Maggie had given her. Photos of all of the Tanner cousins playing together in the snow; of Susannah, Jared, Keith, Seth and Nick all sitting in a row on a sled in a pose much like the one their fathers had been in thirty years before; of Noah and Luke and Tanner standing in front of the Christmas tree; of Jill and Maggie and Tess sitting together on the hearth, of Tanner and Maggie and the boys, of Luke and Jill and Keith.

Of Tess and Susannah and himself.

"Family groups," Maggie had said without a trace of irony. "We can start our own albums."

But, damn it, Noah wanted more than an album full of Christmas memories. He wanted Tess and Susannah all year.

"Daddy?" He heard Susannah calling him from the bedroom. She sounded scared.

He took the stairs two at a time. His leg hurt. He didn't care. "What is it? What's wrong?"

When he appeared in the doorway, the relief on her face was clear. "I—I thought you'd gone." Her voice wavered.

"I told her you were downstairs," Tess said defensively. Then she turned away, going to the closet to hang up one of Susannah's shirts.

"I was bringing in the presents," he said easily. "I'm not goin' anywhere. Not for a while," he went on, for both their benefits. "I've gotta get my leg sorted out first."

Susannah smiled and settled back against the pillows again. "Good."

Tess didn't say a word.

* * *

Not that many days passed until he got a medical all-clear. His leg was mending. "Quicker than we expected," the doctor told him. So he didn't have to go in anymore.

"You just keep working at it wherever you go," the therapist told him.

"And we'll be keeping an eye out for you," the doctor, a rodeo fan, promised. "You take it easy at first, but just go on the way you've been and you'll do fine."

And of course, because they were almost right down the hall from her, they shared the good news with Tess. They thought she'd be pleased.

She was. But not for the reason they suspected.

And when fate somehow decreed that Jim Jackson call that very night on his way to Denver for the stock show and rodeo, Tess said, "Oh, yes, he's all better. I'm sure he'll be ready to go."

So what was he supposed to say? *I'm not?*

"Reckoned you'd be gettin' antsy 'bout now," Jim said cheerfully to Noah when Tess handed him the phone. "I can pick you up on my way down if you want. You ain't too far outa my way."

Noah looked at Tess. She was looking at him. Waiting. Hoping?

He dragged in a harsh breath. Why postpone the inevitable? "All right," he said. "I'll look out for you about ten." He hung up and met Tess's gaze. "I'll be leaving in the morning."

She nodded. "It's about time."

"You're going? Away?" Susannah was standing in the kitchen, her fingers gripped around the back of a chair. Her voice sounded as hollow as his stomach felt. "For good?"

"Of course not," he said briskly. "Now that I know you're here, I'm not just vanishing forever. I'll be back."

"When?"

She would ask that.

He shrugged, turning to pour himself a cup of coffee, his fourth cup this morning, and it wasn't even eight o'clock. "I don't know. My life's not all that regular, you know?"

Of course she didn't know. How could she? She was seven years old. She'd never gone down the road in her life. "Sit down and eat your cereal," he said.

She sat, or rather slumped, in the chair. She didn't look at him.

He scanned the boxes on the top of the refrigerator. "What kind do you want?"

She shrugged and picked up her spoon and idly tapped it on the table. "I'm not hungry."

"You've got to eat breakfast. It's the most important meal of the day."

"Not if you throw it up." The spoon whacked the table-top.

"You're not going to throw it up."

"I might."

Noah thought he might, too—the very thought of leaving was making him ill—but he wasn't going to admit it. "Don't say that. Here. Have some of these corn things."

Susannah made a gagging sound, but she didn't protest when he dumped some cereal into a bowl, sloshed milk on it and set it in front of her. She didn't eat it, either, though she did stir her spoon around in it so that within minutes it became a soggy, unappetizing mess.

"Did you get up to say goodbye to Mommy?"

"Yeah."

Tess had told him last night he didn't have to. She had to be on duty by seven and would be leaving at six-thirty.

"We'll say goodbye tonight," she'd told him briskly just before bedtime. "No sense in you getting up." And then she'd stuck out her hand, shaking his as if he were some vacuum-cleaner salesman she was glad to see hit the road.

Which wasn't that far from the truth, he reflected grimly.

He'd got up anyway. Hell, why not? He hadn't slept all night. He'd lain in her spartan room trying to memorize it all, just like he had last time, so he could take it with him, close his eyes and dream he was in her bed again—in her arms again, as he had been that single wonderful night. The night before reality had come crashing down on him.

He'd got up and come down while she was eating her piece of toast. But if he'd been hoping for a last-minute reprieve, he hadn't got it. She'd outdone herself with cheerful babble, telling him how nice it was that he had mended so well and so quickly, how much he must be looking forward to getting back on the road again, how important it was to do what a person loved to do.

"And you do love it," she'd said firmly.

He'd nodded his head. It was true.

"I love you, too," he'd said.

For an instant she'd looked almost stricken, then she'd turned and grabbed her coat. "I'm going to be late," she said, and without another word, she'd vanished out the door.

He'd stood watching her go, feeling helpless. As helpless as he felt now, watching Susannah muck about miserably with her cereal.

"I've gotta get my gear," he said after a moment, when he couldn't bear watching her any longer. And without another word he bolted out of the kitchen and up the stairs. He'd already packed his duffel bag. He'd borrowed Tanner's old association saddle when they were there for

Christmas. His had needed a bit of work after the crash. He lugged them both downstairs now.

Susannah was sitting on the rocker in the living room. The Christmas tree was gone now. The manger scene that had been on the mantel had been put away. So had the brass candlesticks and the nutcracker that Tess's sister Nancy had brought them from Austria. The room was back to its everyday self.

Life was getting back to its everyday routine—Tess off to work, Susannah to school and Noah going down the road.

"Will you write me?" Susannah asked him.

"Sure."

"Will you call?"

He hesitated. Could he stand the pain of pretending indifference every time he got Tess on the phone?

Susannah noticed his reluctance at once. Her face fell. "It's okay," she said. "You don't have to."

"I want to!" Noah protested. "I love you."

Susannah didn't say anything to that. She just looked at him. Disbelieving? He hoped not, but he didn't know.

There was a beep of a horn outside. "That's Janna," he said. "You've got to go."

Susannah stood up. In one hand she clutched the top of a crumpled paper lunch sack. In the other she carried her backpack. She looked up at him, then ran her tongue over her lips. The lower one quivered. Suddenly she dropped both the sack and the backpack and launched herself at him, grabbing him around the waist.

Noah pulled her up, hugging her against his chest, choking from the tight feeling just beneath the warmth where her small body touched his heart. She kissed him, a great smacking kiss, a desperate kiss. And the one he gave her in return was no less intense.

There was another insistent beep.

"You gotta go," Noah said hoarsely, drawing in one last breath of soft, little-girl scent. And then he set her down.

They looked at each other.

A single tear slid down Susannah's cheek. "I love you," she told him.

"I love you, too," he told her.

"Both of you," he added quietly to himself after she had gone. "More than anything else in the world."

"Figured you'd come," Jim said as he bustled past Noah into the living room and grabbed the saddle sitting by the rocker. "Said to Mike I reckoned you'd be about stir-crazy by now. Hell, you been in one place more'n a month!"

Noah picked up his duffel bag and carried it out. Jim had the back of his pickup open and was tossing the saddle in by the time he got there. He already had his own gear and Mike Hansen's in there, along with their saddles and rigging bags, a couple of sleeping bags, a camp stove and a pair of the biggest speakers Noah had ever seen.

"Pile on in," Mike said, shoving over.

Noah looked over his shoulder at Tess's house. His gaze flicked from the snowman in the front yard—a new one he and Susannah had built just yesterday to replace the one she'd been building the day he'd first learned he had a daughter—to the upstairs window above the front porch, the one in Tess's room—the room where he had lain alone and lonely, the room where he had known a night of perfect love.

"What'sa matter?" Jim asked. "Forget somethin'? Well, if you have, you better think of it right quick 'cause we're movin' out." A wide grin split his face and he rubbed his hands together. "A new year, a new race, a new chance to have it all."

"All?" Noah echoed hollowly, still looking at the house.

Jim and Mike both focused on his gold belt buckle.

"Well, hell, you've already had it, I reckon," Jim said, "but there's plenty of us still hungry. Ain'tcha hungry no more, Noah?"

"Course he is," Mike answered for him. "Noah's always hungry. It's what makes him so damn good. He never quits goin' after the gold."

"'Cause he loves it, don'tcha, Noah?" Jim said. "Loves the challenge. Like you always said—more'n anything else in the world."

There was no Noah in the kitchen. No Noah in the hall.

No Noah sitting in the rocker with his sock-clad feet resting on the hearth, the way he'd been just yesterday.

No Noah anywhere in the house at all.

He was gone. Down the road again, just the way she'd always known he would. Just the way she wanted it.

Or at least she'd thought it was. Until today.

And if she'd hoped that her misgivings would vanish when she opened the front door after work that afternoon, she was disappointed.

She was the only one home.

It was no big surprise. She knew that Susannah had a Brownie meeting after school and that Janna was going to take the girls by Green Acres for a visit afterward. So Susannah would be home by five-thirty. That was only two hours away.

Tess kicked off her shoes, shrugged out of her coat and looked around. She should be relishing the quiet. The peace. Having the place to herself again.

She wasn't.

Because she missed him. Loved him.

She'd driven him away. Now she wanted him back.

"How perverse is that?" she asked Noah-the-cat as she bent down and scratched him under the chin.

He rubbed his head against her leg and purred.

Tess sighed and got to her feet again, then climbed the stairs slowly, unbuttoning the white uniform tunic as she went, peeling it off as she entered the bedroom.

"Well, if you're beginnin' as you mean to go on, we've got a hell of a start."

She almost jumped out of her skin. "Noah!"

He was leaning against the brass headboard of her bed, shirtless, his arms folded behind his head. A slow smile crept across his face as he looked her up and down.

Tess's face flamed. Clutching the tunic in front of her, she glared at him. "I thought you left. You said you were leaving!"

"Nope."

"But—"

"Was goin' to," Noah said. "Then I got to thinking. Somethin' Jim said about why I was good at bronc riding. He said I worked so damned hard at it 'cause I loved it more than I loved anything else." He gave a small shrug. "Yeah, well, it *was* true. It isn't anymore."

Tess stared at him.

"I know you don't believe me," he went on. "You think I'm only sayin' it on account of Susannah. But that isn't true, either. I love Susannah. No question about it. But that's father-daughter stuff. It isn't close to the way I love you, and I'm damned well gonna prove it to you." Now he was almost glaring at her, as if daring her to challenge him.

She ran her tongue over her lips. "Are you?" she said softly. "And how are you going to do that?"

"Perseverance. You aren't gonna be able to get rid of me."

"No?"

He shook his head. "Nope." He moved his head so she could see his hands.

She gaped.

Noah grinned at her. "I figured handcuffin' myself to the bedpost was a pretty good way to start."

It was perhaps not his most-well-thought-out scheme, but it did seem to be getting her attention. Noah was grateful for that. Steve had thought he was nuts when he'd banged on the door this morning asking to borrow a pair of handcuffs once he'd sent Jim and Mike on their way. Maybe it was nuts, but desperate times called for desperate measures. And it was the only thing he could think of to do.

Tess stared, and then she laughed and—damn it to hell— were those tears running down her cheeks? "You're crazy, you know that?" she said finally.

"About you," Noah said earnestly. He leaned as far toward her as he was able. "I'm no good at sweet talk. But I never lied to you, Tess. Not then. Not now. You are the best thing that ever happened to me. I should've seen it years ago. I was too young and too dumb."

"You weren't ready for marriage," Tess murmured.

"Not then. I am now. I'll do the best I can for you—always. Do you believe me?"

Slowly she nodded her head. "I believe you, Noah."

From her purse she pulled out a rumpled copy of *Pro-Rodeo Sports News*. It was folded open to the coming rodeo listings. "I was coming to Denver next weekend after you."

Now it was Noah's turn to stare. "You were? You changed your mind?"

"When you said you loved me, I was afraid to trust you," she admitted. "But then I got to realizing what you told me is true—you don't lie. You've never lied to me, never promised something that you didn't mean. Maggie and Jill said Robert and Luke lied to them and lied to themselves about their feelings. You never have. When you didn't love me, you never told me you did—"

"That's me," Noah said with a snort of self-disgust, "honest as hell."

"I'm glad," Tess told him. "Because when you tell you love me, well, I do believe it."

And then she crossed the room, bent over and touched her lips to his.

He tried to reach for her. He was stuck fast. "Unlock me," he said against her lips.

"What?" She kept on nibbling, teasing.

Noah struggled against his bonds. "Unfasten the cuffs. The key fell down behind the bed."

"Mmm." Tess smiled and kept on kissing him. She settled onto the bed and ran her hands lightly down his chest.

He shivered at her touch. His hands tightened on the brass. "Tesssssss!"

She unfastened the fly of his jeans, easing down the zipper, then tugging the denim down his legs. His briefs quickly followed them.

"Tess!"

She grinned. "This is fun."

"I'll show you fun!" His hips lifted right off the mattress as she ran her hands lightly up the insides of his thighs. He sucked in a sharp breath. "Damn, Tess!"

The grin widened. "Lots of fun."

"For you, maybe," he growled.

She pulled back and looked at him with wide-eyed innocence. "You're not having fun?"

He groaned. "C'mon, Tess."

"I will," she said saucily. "Don't rush me."

But damned if she wasn't rushing him! The things she was doing were driving him wild. Feather-light touches that made him ache. Gentle nips that left him breathless. Warm breath that nearly sent him spinning out of control.

"You want me to suffer," he moaned. "That's why you're doing this."

She settled back on her heels. "Is it? I thought it was because I loved you, too."

He stilled completely, his gaze fixed on her. "Do you mean that?" he asked hoarsely.

She tipped her head. "Do you honestly think I'd be doing this if I didn't?"

Slowly, solemnly, he shook his head. No, there was no way on earth Tess Montgomery would be this intimate with a man unless he meant more to her than any man in the world.

Noah's head dropped back against the pillow. He grinned all over his face. "In that case, sweetheart, go right ahead."

It was interesting, actually, making love with your hands cuffed to a bedpost. He'd sure as hell never done it before.

He wasn't sure he wanted to do it again any time soon.

He didn't mind giving her the control, he just wanted to use his hands. He wanted to touch her, tease her, caress her, bring her to the fever pitch she brought him to before finally unlocking the cuffs and setting him free.

When at last she did, he entered her with one swift, shattering movement. But what he lacked in finesse, he more than made up for in urgency. And he wasn't too worried that Tess would complain. She was exploding in his arms at the very same time.

After, when she lay curled against his chest and he had his arms wrapped around her, he started thinking of other ways he could make love to her—with her—now that he had the time, and the future, to try them all. He smiled in anticipation.

"You know what you told Susannah," he said softly, his lips against her hair, "about how cowboys always move on?"

Tess lifted her head and nodded slowly.

"Well, it ain't so." He touched his lips to hers. "Not always. Not when they smarten up, anyway." He grinned. "This cowboy's here to stay."

Epilogue

One year later

It was, just as Tanner had said last year, "wall-to-wall rug rats" again this Christmas at the Three Bar C ranch. But this year Noah was here to see it—he and Tess and Susannah, a family at last. Noah surveyed the chaos in the living room with a smile on his face.

Seth and Nick, approaching the terrible twos, were shredding bags of discarded wrapping paper, their presents paling in the light of such great sport. Keith was sitting in the middle of the floor sucking his thumb and contemplating a Keith-size rolling horsey that Jared was pushing around and around, making race-car noises.

Susannah, God bless her, was curled in the corner of the sofa, absorbed in a stack of *Black Stallion* books her aunt Maggie and uncle Robert had given her. It was the first time she'd settled down in the house since Noah and Tess had taken her out to the barn that morning to show her the two-year-old black gelding who'd been waiting just for her. She'd been stunned. Amazed.

"He's beautiful," she'd cried. "Better than even my bike." And they hadn't been able to get her into the house until Noah had gone out and dragged her in when dinner was on the table.

An angry wail from upstairs reminded Noah that there was even one more rug rat this time around—a girl, Katharine Elizabeth, called Katie, born to Luke and Jill in August.

"Reinforcements," Susannah had called her only girl cousin, and she'd breathed a deep sigh of relief. The news of Katie's arrival hadn't stopped her from pestering her parents, however.

"I really could use a sister," she'd told Noah and Tess on more than one occasion after their marriage last February. "Or even a brother," she'd allowed, though she'd wrinkled her nose as she said it. "You know, it isn't good for a girl to be an only child."

They'd smiled then, but they hadn't committed themselves.

Now, of course, with Tess waddling around as big as Tanner's old red barn, neither of them had to say a word.

God, she was beautiful, Noah thought as he studied Tess's freckled cheeks, which had turned rosy in the heat of the room. He smiled just looking at her. Her curves were so different now that she was full with his child. He'd loved to touch her when she was lithe and lissome, but no more than he delighted in running his hands over her now. It was all he could do not to walk right out into the living room and—

"Hey!" Tanner's voice broke into his reverie. "If you figure standin' over there by the door and lookin' the other way is gonna keep you from having to dry your share of these dishes, buster, you're dead wrong."

Noah turned just in time to catch the snap of a damp dish towel against the seat of his jeans. "Hey, yourself! I was just thinking."

Tanner saw what—or who—his brother was looking at and gave him a knowing grin. "Sure you were. Reckon Tess is gettin' sort of tomatolike in that red dress," he added cheerfully.

"She is not!"

At the ferocity of Noah's tone, Tanner broke up, laughing.

Luke, elbow deep in soapsuds, joined in. "God, you're easy to tease," he said as Noah bristled.

"Just like old times," Tanner agreed. He turned to Luke. "You remember when he was nuts about that mangy ol' yellow dog?"

Noah was across the kitchen in a tenth of a second flat, ready to commit mayhem. "That dog was not...!"

But Tanner was grinning his head off again. So was Luke.

"Aw, hell," Noah muttered.

Tanner poked him in the ribs. "It was the prettiest damn dog in Colorado," he admitted, thirty years too late.

"It was," Noah agreed gruffly.

"And Tess is one heck of a tomato," Tanner said. He aimed an appreciative glance in her direction.

"Sure is," Luke said. "You're damned lucky to have her."

"I know it," Noah said softly. He told himself that every day of his life.

"Reckon we're all lucky," Tanner said, catching sight of his own lovely Maggie just coming down the stairs.

"Uh-huh," Luke said. He wiped his hands on the legs of his jeans and turned to stand shoulder to shoulder with his brothers as they all three contemplated the women—and the children—who had brought such joy into their lives. "Damn lucky."

And Noah, remembering Susannah's prayer last Christmas, sent one of thanksgiving in the same direction now. Then he swallowed against the lump in his throat.

"Nope," he said, with a catch in his voice that his brothers politely—and uncharacteristically—ignored. "We've been way more than lucky. We've been blessed."

*   *   *   *   *

Noah Tanner's best friend and rodeo buddy, Taggart Jones, gets more female company than he expects when he leaves the rodeo circuit and settles down to be a full-time father to his little girl, Becky. Look for Taggart's story, THE COWBOY AND THE KID by Anne McAllister, coming from Silhouette Desire in summer 1996.

COMING NEXT MONTH

#973 WOLFE WEDDING—Joan Hohl

Big Bad Wolfe
No one ever thought January's *Man of the Month*, Cameron Wolfe, was the marrying kind. But a romantic getaway with brainy beauty Sandra Bradley suddenly had the lone wolf thinking about a Wolfe wedding!

#974 MY HOUSE OR YOURS?—Lass Small

The last thing Josephine Morris wanted was to let her infuriating ex, Chad Wilkins, permanently back into her life. Yet when he proposed they have a wild, romantic *affair*, Jo just couldn't say no....

#975 LUCAS: THE LONER—Cindy Gerard

Sons and Lovers
Lucas Caldwell knew better than to trust the sultry reporter who suddenly appeared on his ranch. But Kelsey Gates wouldn't stop until she got her story—or her man!

#976 PEACHY'S PROPOSAL—Carole Buck

Wedding Belles
Peachy Keene just wasn't going to live her life as a virgin! So she proposed a no-strings affair with dashing Luke Devereaux—and got much more than she bargained for.

#977 COWBOY'S BRIDE—Barbara McMahon

Single dad Trace Longford would do anything to make new neighbor Kalli Bonotelli sell her ranch to him. But now the rugged cowboy not only wanted her ranch—he wanted Kalli, too!

#978 SURRENDER—Metsy Hingle

Aimee Lawrence had found Mr. Right—but he insisted she sign a prenuptial agreement! Now he had to prove his feelings for her ran much deeper than lust—or there would be *no* wedding....

MILLION DOLLAR SWEEPSTAKES (III)

INTRODUCING…

A collection of award-winning books by award-winning authors! From Harlequin and Silhouette.

Falling Angel
by Anne Stuart

WINNER OF THE RITA AWARD FOR BEST ROMANCE!

Falling Angel by Anne Stuart is a RITA Award winner, voted Best Romance. A truly wonderful story, *Falling Angel* will transport you into a world of hidden identities, second chances and the magic of falling in love.

"Ms. Stuart's talent shines like the brightest of stars, making it very obvious that her ultimate destiny is to be the next romance author at the top of the best-seller charts."
—*Affaire de Coeur*

A heartwarming story for the holidays. You won't want to miss award-winning *Falling Angel*, available this January wherever Harlequin and Silhouette books are sold.

It's our 1000th Special Edition and we're celebrating!

Join us these coming months for some wonderful stories in a special celebration of our 1000th book with some of your favorite authors!

Diana Palmer   **Nora Roberts**
Debbie Macomber   **Christine Flynn**
Phyllis Halldorson   **Lisa Jackson**

Plus miniseries by:

Lindsay McKenna, Marie Ferrarella, Sherryl Woods and Gina Ferris Wilkins.

And many more books by special writers!

And as a special bonus, all Silhouette Special Edition titles published during Celebration 1000! will have _**double**_ Pages & Privileges proofs of purchase!

Silhouette Special Edition...heartwarming stories packed with emotion, just for you! You'll fall in love with our next 1000 special stories!

1000BK-R

You're About to Become a

Privileged Woman

Reap the rewards of fabulous free gifts and
benefits with proofs-of-purchase from
Silhouette and Harlequin books

Pages & Privileges™

It's our way of thanking you for
buying our books at your
favorite retail stores.

**Harlequin and Silhouette—
the most privileged readers in the world!**

For more information about Harlequin and
Silhouette's PAGES & PRIVILEGES program call the
Pages & Privileges Benefits Desk: 1-503-794-2499

SD-PP8